THE MAGMA PROPHECY

BY ALAN ZEMEK

Cover Art by Lily Jerome
Interior Illustration by Ed Worry
Publication Design & Production by ocreations, llc.

ISBN: 978-0-9960921-3-5

For my family

⟨⟩ CHAPTER 1 ⟨⟩

Five, four, three —the voice counted down. "Let me out of here!" AJ screamed. His face was white as he pounded on the tube's smooth wet sides. Through the rushing water he could just barely see his friend Kay across the way. He yelled again, but she didn't reply. Then the last number echoed in the tube —*One!* He heard a gurgle, a whoosh, and then a deafening roar! She was gone. He thought this was the end.

He was falling—and falling fast. Water was all around him, pushing him down. He felt his thin body twist as the track changed direction. Then suddenly he was outside, floating on his back, feeling the sun's rays. He tentatively opened his eyes. As his vision adjusted, he saw Kay crawling out from the adjacent tube. She was beaming.

"That was the best waterslide ever!" She wrung out her long brown braid as she made her way over to AJ. "You okay? You look a little pale."

AJ steadied himself and pulled up his lanky frame. His cropped hair was already almost dry. He paused and looked serious. "I don't want to ever do that again." They both laughed. "Let's go find Jack and Eagle. I need some funnel cake!"

Kay and AJ walked away from the "The Flush" waterslide. They smiled as they relived the experience in their minds.

The four friends were still on their summer break. They were celebrating having completed their big adventure over the past few months, preventing a disaster predicted by an ancient legend.

Kay's older brother Jack and their friend Eagle were checking out the carnival games. Jack had won several big prizes and was rewarding himself by buying a pretzel from a cart. Eagle's flip-flops slapped as he turned to greet Kay and AJ.

"Can you believe it? That's the third stuffed animal already," Eagle called. "He's like a machine."

"Basketball toss?" AJ asked.

"Oh yeah. It's got to be that. Right?" Kay smiled.

Eagle nodded. "You got it. He showed me the trick." Eagle mimed an underhand throw. "It's not very manly, but it really works. That, and his linebacker size, gives him a big advantage."

Jack joined the others. The pretzel he was chewing muffled his words. "Hey, I've been showing Eagle how to throw the ball so it lands in the basket. Underhand, high arc, and banked off the backboard. I think he's getting the hang of it. Check out these prizes." Jack held up two rattlesnakes and a tarantula.

"Those are perfect for you, Jack," AJ laughed. "Good thing they're fake."

"You said it." Jack shivered at the thought of real ones.

"Hey, I won this little bunny." Eagle held up the cute fur ball and flashed his bright smile.

"Great," Kay scoffed. "You too can spend two dollars on a ticket to win a forty-cent stuffed animal."

"It's the thrill of victory." Eagle high-fived Jack. His palm stung from the solid slap. "And it's always good to have a skill." He shook out his hand and looked at Kay. "You want a prize, don't you?"

"Me? No," she protested.

"You do," Eagle teased. "Come on..."

Kay blushed. "Yeah. Okay. I guess I do," she smiled. "Can you win one?"

Eagle reached for his colorful cloth wallet and handed the money over to the attendant.

"Remember, Eagle." Jack offered some last-minute coaching. "Just like we practiced."

Eagle pushed back his long black hair, then held the basketball in his hands and spun it backward, gauging its weight and feel. The others looked on with anticipation as he lined up the shot. Focusing on the backboard, he bent his elbows, then flung his wrists forward, creating backspin. As the ball traveled, it looked like a perfect shot. It hit the backboard, angled down toward the rim, bounced twice, and then spun off to the side. Eagle shook his head, embarrassed. He'd really wanted to win this one for Kay.

"Don't worry." Kay put her hand on Eagle's shoulder. "I've seen Jack miss a million times." Eagle shrugged off his disappointment and smiled back.

Kay beckoned everyone to follow her. "Let's check out Devil's Drop."

The four moved toward Devil's Drop but stopped briefly at a funnel cake stand. The smell of frying was everywhere. When the bubbling batter turned crisp and golden, the cook removed it from the "fry daddy" with a slotted metal skimmer. He placed the funnel cake on a paper plate. AJ dabbed the cake a few times with a napkin, shook on some powdered sugar, and smacked his lips. But before he had time to take a bite, Jack ripped off a piece. He grinned as he ate.

"Thanks for leaving me some," AJ joked.

"No problem." Jack put his arm around AJ. "You know I couldn't resist. Come on, the ride's this way."

"There's no way I'm going on that thing." AJ shook his head emphatically. "That's like a hundred-foot drop with just a bungee cord or something."

"AJ. It looks less scary than 'The Flush.'" Kay tried to encourage him.

"It reminds me of rock climbing, hundreds of feet above a river valley with nothing but a rope. I'm not you, Kay. Not everyone lives for this stuff," AJ explained.

They all nodded, remembering AJ's issues with heights.

Kay gave in. "Okay. But you should get some good photos of us while we're falling."

"That I can do."

They carefully read the warning sign: *Do not go on this ride if you have a fear of heights, a heart condition, a back condition, or any other ailment that might cause you to freak out while being hurled a hundred feet down toward the ground!*

Good luck and have fun!

"Eagle. Are you up for this? I know Jack is."

"I wouldn't miss it for the world." Eagle masked his anxiety. He didn't want Kay to see he was really scared.

Kay looked at Jack. "Are you in?"

"I guess." He shrugged.

"Good luck, guys. I'll take some good shots. Try to smile—and breathe." AJ laughed.

The three friends climbed the steps up a hundred feet to the platform. Kay scaled a few at a time with her long legs. "Man, we're pretty high up." She moved to the edge. "Check it out! You can see the whole town. I think that's our house," she pointed. "And there's Dad's restaurants."

"What's that?" Jack pointed to small flashes of light coming from the center of town.

"That's the wind sculpture. It's spinning so fast," Kay marveled.

"That's awesome." Jack surveyed the landscape. "Check out The Spires." Jack pointed to the rock outcroppings in front of Mount Fuego on the horizon. "They're so tall."

"Have you climbed them?" Eagle asked.

"I wish," Kay sighed. "There's no trail up there. Too remote."

"Hey, move back, kid," the ride attendant called. "You're too close to the edge. You're making me nervous."

She took one more look and stepped back.

The attendant fitted each of them with a harness and clipped them together with metal carabiners. They caught sight of AJ waving below. They were attached to a cord suspended from a steel crane that stretched out overhead for fifty feet. When they jumped into the open air, they would freefall, swinging like pendulums, over the man-made lake below.

"Maybe I don't want to do this," Jack joked.

"Too late," Kay shot back. "There's only one way down from here and that's straight off." She peered around Jack to see how Eagle was holding up. He was quiet. "It'll be over soon," she assured him. "It'll be fun—you'll see."

Eagle tried to grin.

"Are you guys ready?" the attendant asked.

"Yes!" Kay said the loudest.

On the count of three, they jumped. AJ watched from below. After the initial straight drop, the bungee cord pulled tight, slowing their descent and arcing them toward the middle of the lake. AJ snapped a photo right as they swooped close to the water. He could hear Jack screaming in excitement as they swung back and forth.

As she bounced up and back, Kay coolly scanned the entire park, focusing on the people. She tilted her head, confused, as she noticed many of them were on their knees. Finally the friends' speed slowed, and they landed on the lower platform next to the water's edge. AJ made his way over.

"That was amazing!" Kay shouted. She looked over to Eagle to see if he was okay.

"Wow!" he exclaimed. The wind had made his eyes water, and tears glazed his bronze cheeks. "Everything was moving so fast. It's good to be back on solid ground." Eagle unhooked himself and stood on the platform with Kay and Jack. "Hey, I still feel like things are moving." Eagle tried to steady his legs.

"I can't get my balance either." Kay swiveled to check her friends and then glanced out across the park. The ground seemed to rock, and people were running and falling. She heard rumbling and screaming, but she couldn't tell if it was coming from the rides or something else.

"It's an earthquake!" AJ yelled. He struggled to make his way over. "Quick!" He motioned for them to move to an open area away from the rides. As they were running to safety, the screaming got louder, and they dodged people scrambling in all directions. Jack led the way as the others rode in his wake. When the shaking finally stopped, they all steadied themselves.

"That was intense," Eagle exhaled. He sized everyone up and looked back at Devil's Drop. "It's a good thing we just got off that thing. We were pretty lucky." The park attendants were still helping people off the other rides and directing them to open areas.

"Another earthquake?" Jack turned to AJ. "You're the science genius. What's going on? Isn't that like third one in the past few weeks?"

"I think you're right." AJ knelt down and touched the ground. "And that was a big one." He wondered what was going on inside the Earth.

"Is this area even supposed to have these things?" Jack questioned.

"We should go," Kay directed, sternly scanning the area. People were calming down, and there didn't appear to be any major damage. She noticed that one of the rides had lost power. "They're going to close the park. They'll have to check everything."

Just then they heard a park-wide announcement confirming Kay's prediction. They all frowned.

"I guess that's smart." Eagle perked up. He thought about the free-fall drop he had just experienced, then the added thrill of getting off onto moving ground. "That was wild!" He grinned at his friends. People were filing to the exits. He tapped Jack on the arm. "Glad we're all safe and sound, but I'm not ready to stop our celebration. Hey, it's still early. Maybe we can get some real food at your father's new place? Best BBQ in New Mexico. Right?"

Jack's eyes lit up. "You bet! Ribs. Mac and cheese. Corn bread. I'm starving."

"That's a shocker," Kay laughed.

"Hey, that sounds good," AJ agreed.

"I'm in," Kay nodded. "Let's get our bikes and go."

⊛ CHAPTER 2 ⊛

As they rode up the dirt road just outside their small town, hickory smoke wafted over a hill. They were nearing Fiery Bill's. Kay and Jack's father had opened this place a few weeks ago, building on the success of his first restaurant, El Chico Loco.

Fiery Bill's was an open-pit BBQ joint with a selection of fifteen specialty sauces ranging from mild to scorching—go to the hospital—hot!

The place had a down-home feel, with indoor and outdoor seating. There was a large patio where the smoker stood next to the kitchen. Picnic tables were covered with fresh paper tablecloths. The BBQ sauce was messy, so the staff changed the paper for every new customer. As they walked in, the hostess, Marisa, greeted them. "Hey guys. Did you feel all the shaking?"

"We were at the park, and it hit right as we got off Devil's

Drop," Jack said. "It was wild. I couldn't tell if it was me or the ground that was still moving."

"Well, lucky for us there's no damage here. Just some knocked-over water glasses." Marisa looked at the patio tables, then back at Jack. "Hey, can you work a shift after you guys eat? We're short right now."

"Sure," Jack replied.

"Great. I'll let everyone know." Marisa collected some menus and pointed to an open table on the patio right next to the kitchen window. "Take that one," she directed. Since they were family, she gave them a table too noisy for most regular customers.

Jack nodded and grabbed the menus. They all walked over to sit.

"Well, I'm getting the usual." Jack put the menu down.

"The Trifecta?" Kay asked.

"Yeah. But I'm going with the Hungry Man today."

"Three racks of ribs, mac and cheese, and corn bread?" She rolled her eyes. "Where do you put it?"

"Makes me tall—and strong." Jack laughed.

"You're already both of those," she commented.

Jack flexed his biceps and smiled. "I think I'm going to try this sauce again." He flicked his finger on the menu.

"That's 'The Heart Attack'!" Eagle read the description. "Wow! Ghost peppers, habeneros, and jalapenos all in one sauce. I think you need to sign something to eat it."

They all laughed.

"It's not too bad," Jack shrugged. "You want to try?"

"Sure," Eagle said confidently. "Bring it on."

"Eagle. That's pretty hot," Kay cautioned. "Don't let him

bait you."

"It's okay. I'm good with hot food. My grandfather makes a killer chili that we always take to our Native American festivals. It's really hot, too."

"I don't think you understand." Kay rolled her eyes.

Jack made his way over to the squeeze bottles of BBQ sauces at the counter. They were lined up from mild to hot. He selected a few, including "The Heart Attack," from the hot side.

Moments later, the food arrived.

"Who's first?" AJ asked.

"You're up, Jack," Kay instructed. She moved a fresh glass of water toward him. Jack squeezed "The Heart Attack" sauce onto the side of his plate. It was thick and fiery red.

Kay and AJ smiled as they watched.

"Okay. Let's do it!" Jack picked up a rib, dipped it in the sauce, and then placed it in his mouth. Sweat streamed down his forehead and his eyes watered. He grabbed a napkin and wiped his face.

"Here we go again." Kay shook her head. "It's just like when you eat burritos, Jack. I don't know why you eat these hot dishes if they make you sweat so much." She looked around the restaurant, embarrassed, making sure she didn't know anyone.

"I'm in serious pain." He sniffled as his nose started to run. He reached for the tall glass of water. "But it tastes so good. I can't stop eating it!" He smiled, exhaled deeply, and then grabbed another rib.

Everyone laughed.

"You're up, Eagle." Kay pushed the bottle over. "You

sure you want to do this?"

Eagle was a little nervous, but he knew he had to do it. "I'm ready." He squeezed the sauce liberally on his plate, grabbed a rib, and dipped it. "Well, here goes nothing." He placed it in his mouth.

When the fiery sauce hit his tongue, Eagle's eyes grew wide. He paused. Suddenly, his face turned beet red. "*Ahhhhh!*" He fumbled for his water. His eyes filled with tears. He was sweating even more than Jack had.

"Are you okay?" Kay asked. She knew it was nothing serious, but he was in definite pain.

"Hot! Hot!" Eagle fanned his mouth. He danced around the table. "My mouth is on fire! *Ahhhhh!*" he yelled again.

"We need a 'cool down' here." Kay waved at Marisa. She pointed to Eagle.

"Got it, Kay," Marisa shot back. "Cool down, Table Five, coming up!" All the customers turned to check out the commotion.

The restaurant had experience with this sort of emergency. Within seconds a large bowl of vanilla ice cream appeared in front of Eagle. Wasting no time, he shoveled a large spoonful into his mouth. The friends could almost hear the hiss as the cooling ice cream spread over his tongue. He panted heavily and scooped up more. A relieved look crossed his face. The ice cream was slowly bringing his taste buds back to normal.

"That's on the house." Marisa smiled.

Eagle stuck out his tongue. "That's hot." He slurred his words. "I don't know how you do it, Jack." He reached for more water.

Jack patted him on the back. "You're tough, Eagle—really tough. Most people wouldn't even try."

Kay and AJ high-fived Eagle, and several customers clapped. "Nice job!" one called out. Eagle smiled, reached for a napkin, and pushed his long hair back. He slumped down in his chair, slightly embarrassed. "I think I'll stick with something more mild."

They enjoyed their meals in silence for a few moments.

"Hey, check out the TVs," Eagle mumbled and pointed. His mouth was still a bit numb. "That's the park."

"What's with all the recent seismic tremors? Why all the shaking? Scientists are working on a theory... And you're going to want to hear it. Details at five!"

"We have to wait till five o'clock to find out what's going on?" AJ mocked the news report. "That's crazy." He wiped the BBQ sauce from his hands.

"I'm sure you can figure it out on your own," Kay said. "Just look it up online."

"Good point." He nodded, then squirted some fresh sauce on his plate.

They ate their food and watched the TVs. The friends were all stuffed. After demolishing his meal, Jack pushed his chair back, wiped his face, and stood up.

"Okay, I'm fueled up and ready for work." Jack scanned the patio for Marisa. "You heading home?"

Kay nodded.

"Okay, I'm going to work here for the next few hours. Let Dad know, and I'll see you later." Jack tucked in his shirt and went to the front of the restaurant. His face lit up as he started chatting up the customers.

"He's so good at that," Kay said admiringly. She turned to AJ and Eagle. "What a smooth talker."

The others laughed.

"We ready here?" Kay pushed her chair back. They collected their plates and trays. The food was free, but they always paid for the service. After leaving a nice tip on the table, Kay, AJ, and Eagle exited the restaurant and rode away.

They turned off the dirt road to take a shortcut toward home. Their bikes kicked up dust on the loose gravel. Sagebrush dotted the surrounding plateau. As they rode around several red clay rock outcroppings, Kay spotted something unusual. She pulled over.

"What's up?" Eagle asked.

Kay dismounted. Large rocks were scattered at the base of a steep hill. "These boulders are new. Maybe the earthquake knocked them down." She scampered over them and up the hill.

"Kay. What's going on?" AJ got off his bike and walked toward her. "Where are you going?" He huffed as he hustled to catch up.

"Guys, check this out!" she shouted. "Get up here. It's so clear."

"What's so clear?" AJ asked. "You're killin' me here with all this climbing." He reluctantly scrambled up. Eagle followed.

"That!" She pointed.

"Wow!" Eagle stepped back. He gazed at where Kay was pointing. "That's amazing!"

AJ looked, too. "Holy cow! I've never seen anything like it." His mouth was open. "We've got to check this out."

⊛ CHAPTER 3 ⊛

"It looks like a huge zipper—on the ground." AJ climbed higher to see its full length. "I think it's a fault line."

They all looked down. Ridges of earth rippled along the sides of a clearly defined crack on the desert floor.

"It goes that way"— Kay pointed—"to that hill and those rocks." She scanned the horizon. "Let's check it out."

The three friends followed Kay's lead. They climbed down the rock formation and rode their bikes along the newly formed fault line. It ran for about a mile to an isolated hill, where it tunneled inside.

"We're in the middle of nowhere." Kay reached for her phone. There was no reception. She searched for the flashlight app. "We're going in."

"What?" AJ protested. "We're going in?"

Kay surveyed the opening and the hillside above. "Come on, AJ. We were in more dangerous places just a couple weeks ago." She pounded the rock above the entrance. "It looks stable," she said confidently. "We'll just take a quick peek. Eagle, you coming?"

"Oh yeah. This looks awesome. Come on, AJ. Let's go."

AJ slumped. He was nervous but eager to see what was inside. He prodded the rocks around the opening and tugged on some exposed roots. "It does look pretty safe. Let's just take it slow. Okay?"

"Okay," Kay agreed.

She switched on her flashlight app and squeezed through the tight opening. AJ and Eagle followed close behind. To their surprise, the tunnel immediately widened. Wood beams propped up the ceiling as the passage penetrated into the mountain. The beams looked old; some of them were cracked.

"Wow! This is incredible!" Eagle exclaimed. He stepped over a thick beam that had fallen. "What is this place?"

Curiosity lured them on, especially AJ. The faint light from the entrance still lit the interior walls. He touched one of the beams. Rivets made it strong. "Looks like an old mine. I've never heard of this place. Eagle, have you?"

"My grandfather has mentioned ancient tribal mining before—y'know, like from hundreds of years ago— but I've never seen anything like this."

"Talon knows about ancient mining? Maybe we'll find some gold." Kay hoped something shiny would reflect her flashlight. As they moved deeper, the light from the entrance faded. Kay turned to find AJ but couldn't see him in the dark. A wave of nervousness broke over her. "AJ!" she shouted. "Where are you?"

"I'm right here." AJ was just a few yards behind. He

breathed heavily, trying to catch up. Only the silhouette of Kay's face was visible from her phone light.

"What were you doing back there? Stay close," she scolded.

"I was just checking the water coming out of the cracks." AJ moved next to her. "See. It's so warm." He placed his hand on the wall, which was slimy.

Kay shook her head. "Stay together in here. I don't want to get separated. Eagle, you too. I'm the only one with a light." She motioned everyone to regroup.

They pressed deeper into the mountain behind Kay. The shaft banked right, then left.

"It's really hot in here," AJ worried. He motioned to the others to stop. "And I think I hear running water." He felt the wet walls again. "I'm not sure, but I think we're right on the fault line." He shook the warm moisture off his hand. "There must be an underground spring around here."

"Like a hot spring?" Eagle asked.

"Yes. There must be hot magma right under us, heating up the water." AJ grabbed Kay's arm. "Maybe we should turn back?"

"It is pretty hot. I didn't expect this passage to go on so long," Kay admitted nervously. "My phone's dying. You're right! Let's go."

Eagle looked into the blackness of the passage ahead. The air felt hot and the sound of flowing water was getting louder. "Maybe another time." He looked to Kay and AJ. "Let's head out."

They turned for the exit. Just as they took the first step back, a low rumbling echoed through the shaft. The sound intensified and bits of rock fell. Kay's eyes grew wide. "What's going on?" She clutched the sidewall.

AJ moved next to her, and they both stood plastered against the rock. Suddenly debris was flying everywhere, illuminated only by the narrow beam from her phone.

"I think it's another earthquake." AJ covered his mouth with his shirt to avoid breathing in dust.

"Just sit tight," Kay instructed. She swept her light beam down the shaft but couldn't make out Eagle in the cloud of fine particles. "Eagle. Take cover!" she shouted into the gloom. She tried to project calm although her heart was racing. The rumbling grew more intense. The wooden ceiling beams started to crack. "We need to get out of here!" Her hands trembled. Rock was falling from above, and she knew the ceiling was going to cave in. Suddenly a deep crack opened in the wall that she and AJ had been clutching. She pushed AJ in its direction.

"What are you doing?" he yelled.

"Get in the crack, AJ!" she snapped. "Do it now!"

"I don't want to," he protested. He braced himself in the opening, blocking it off.

"Too bad." She pushed him hard and followed close behind. Eagle appeared out of the dust, running toward Kay's light. "Eagle! We're in here!" He ran over and the three of them squeezed in. A shower of debris rained down. Thunderous noise echoed everywhere. They cowered as the main shaft became blocked off. A pile of rock filled it to the ceiling. They were cut off.

After a few moments, the rumbling stopped.

Kay coughed. Bits of dust were suspended in the air.

She flashed her dimming light over the passage. She climbed out of the crack. "We're okay," she reassured herself as well as the others. "For now." She inspected the cave-in.

"We've got to get out of here." AJ's voice fluttered. "This is really bad."

"Hold it together, AJ. Just relax," Kay soothed. "Eagle, are you all right?" Kay asked.

He nodded and walked over to the wall of debris. Copying AJ, he breathed through his shirt to keep out the dust. He tried to muscle aside some fallen rocks, but they would not budge. He exhaled. "I guess we'll have to go this way." He pointed deeper into the mountain. "Hopefully it leads out."

"What are we going to do?" AJ's voice cracked.

"It'll be okay, AJ." Kay looked at her phone. There was still no reception. She shone her light at AJ. "We're not hurt. That's good, right? We'll have to move deeper to see if the passage comes out somewhere. What else can we do?"

"How can you be so calm?" AJ asked, stunned.

"I'm not calm," she shot back. "I'm scared. But we need to think clearly about how to get out of here. And that starts now." She motioned for AJ to start walking. "Let's go."

As the three friends made their way down the dark corridor, the temperature continued to rise, and the sound of flowing water became more intense.

"Maybe something's up ahead," Eagle said hopefully.

The passageway banked right, and as they turned, they noticed a glow. "There's light!" AJ exclaimed. "Maybe we can get out."

Now that there was light, Kay switched off her phone. There was still a little charge left.

AJ rushed forward to see what was at the end of the tunnel, but rocks blocked his path. The friends had to contort their bodies around the debris. They slid around a huge boulder, and a wave of heat enveloped them. They found themselves in a sunlit room.

⊛ CHAPTER 4 ⊛

"**W**ow—look at that!" Kay exclaimed. "What is it?" The room they had entered was hot as an oven. The heat came from a glowing red pit. Over it, hanging from a stone tripod, was a red-hot cauldron. It straddled the pit of thick glowing liquid.

"AJ, what's that hot stuff?" Eagle asked. "It looks like The Heart Attack sauce."

"I think it's lava," AJ marveled. "Melted rock all the way from the center of the Earth—the stuff that comes out of volcanoes. It's really, really hot."

AJ approached the glowing metal pot cautiously. He peered inside. "There's liquid metal in here." Waves of heat radiated up from the lava pit beneath.

"Metal?" Kay raced over. "Like silver or gold? If it is, we're rich!" Kay exulted. "That is, if we can get out of this place." She looked around for an exit.

"It could be silver." AJ studied its color. "Or it could be a mixture. It's hard to say. But there's a lot of it in here." The metal slowly bubbled in the cauldron.

"Hey guys," Eagle called. "Check this out." He pointed to the wall behind the cauldron. On it was a mural. Although it was faded, it clearly showed a flat-topped mountain in front and several tall peaks behind it. On the mountain were four small buildings surrounding a larger one. A crack in the mural ran through the largest building, obscuring it. Water seeped through the crack and pooled on a ledge above and behind the cauldron. Kay reached for her phone and snapped a picture. The room was bright enough that there was no flash. When she looked around for the source of the light, she noticed beams entering through an airshaft above. The opening was wide enough to crawl through, but the walls leading up to it were smooth and arched inward.

Meanwhile, AJ was scrambling around the lava pit to inspect the crack in the mural. With its sharp edges, the crack looked new. "I think all the shaking just opened this up." He extended his hand toward the dripping water. It was warm. Overflowing the ledge, the water drained into a large, jagged hole in the floor.

"The water's going straight down. It's not backing up at all." AJ moved in closer. "Kay, give me your light." He leaned down to investigate.

"Where's it going?" Kay asked. "What's under there?"

"Magma," AJ said. "Y'know—liquid rock inside the Earth. When it comes out it's called lava." AJ stood up to pull away from wisps of steam rising from the hole.

"Check out that glow!" Eagle stared at the cauldron.

"How is it doing that?"

"I read about this type of stuff near a fault line," AJ recalled. "This must be a hot spot. Given how hot the floor is and that glow down in the hole, I'd guess that there's a river of magma right under our feet."

"That is so cool." Eagle eyed the floor.

"Definitely cool." AJ grew nervous. "But not cool—if you know what I mean. We're lucky that most of the steam and heat are venting out the top. Still, magma's unstable. Something dangerous could happen. We need to get out—soon."

They all scanned the room, looking for an exit.

"There!" AJ yelled. He crossed to a heap of rocks piled along a wall. It was on the opposite side of the air vent that Kay had been considering. The rocks formed a rough staircase. Shadows and darkness prevented him from seeing what was on top. "Maybe it's a way out," he hoped. He climbed up and flashed the phone's light at a small opening dug into the sidewall right under the ceiling. "Hey guys! It's another chamber!" he called.

"Does it lead out?" Eagle asked from the bottom of the rock pile.

AJ ducked to enter the chamber, which was small and dark. He crawled in. He swept his light beam over the bare stone walls. "Darn it!" he yelled. "There's no exit."

"Get back down here, AJ," Kay shouted. "Let's stick together. We need to figure a way out."

AJ stooped to exit, but something caught his eye. He moved closer and flashed the light at it. On the floor were two stone cylinders, each about a foot long. One was narrow, and the other was wide. In the dim light, the wide one looked like a sleeping bag stuffed into a sack. He crawled over to investigate.

He reached for the narrow cylinder. To his surprise, it was split into halves, each hollowed out like a canoe. The insides were covered with bumps and grooves. "I'm taking these," he muttered. He put them in his backpack. The other cylinder was also split into hollow halves, but he decided it was too big and heavy to take with him. He snapped a picture of it, and he crawled back out toward the main chamber and the others.

"Find anything?" Kay asked as AJ reappeared.

"Just some cool rocks." AJ lugged his backpack containing the stone cylinder down the rock staircase. The weight made the pack cut into his shoulders.

Meanwhile, Kay had been surveying the walls of the chamber. There was no doorway other than the one through which they had entered. She studied the light entering through the large airshaft. "Up and out. Looks like the only way."

"That's like twenty feet up, Kay. I can't climb up there," AJ protested. "We don't have any of your climbing gear."

Kay slumped. "You're right." She walked over and felt the sloping walls leading up to the shaft. They were smooth. "Not enough hand holds, plus it's an overhang."

Just then, they all heard a loud *crackle* and *hiss*. The noises echoed off the walls. Suddenly, bits of metal were flying everywhere.

"Take cover!" Kay shouted, confused. She and AJ huddled behind a boulder while Eagle dove down the entrance passage.

Water was now surging through the crack in the mural and spilling into the cauldron. As it hit the hot metal, it flashed into steam, like water in a hot frying pan. The metal spattered over the room.

"I'm scared," AJ yelled. They couldn't risk moving to where Eagle had taken shelter for fear of being ripped by the flying metal shards.

"Just keep your head down, AJ." Kay sought to reassure him although she knew the situation was dire. They both cowered, flinching every time the molten metal popped.

"Don't move, guys!" Eagle shouted over the deafening noise. "I have an idea." If he could divert the water's flow from the cauldron, the hot metal bits would stop flying out. He retraced his steps down the passage to the cave-in. He looked for large but light stones to throw. He hurriedly collected as many as he could, then rushed back.

"Keep your heads down, guys. I got this," Eagle shouted. He dumped the stones at his feet. Sizing up the distance, he grabbed a stone and threw it toward the shelf. It flew into the streaming water but caromed off the ledge.

"What are you doing?" Kay yelled. Peering around the boulder, through the steam, dust, and flying metal, she could only make out Eagle's arm waving back and forth.

Undeterred, Eagle grabbed another stone. "Concentrate," he told himself. He threw, and this time the stone stuck on the shelf. It didn't divert the water, but maybe more stones would. He raced out of the room to resupply.

"I'm sorry, AJ," Kay said over the crackling. "I shouldn't have made you come in here. I'm so sorry." She looked away.

"It's not your fault." He flinched as more hot metal shards

ricocheted off the walls. He shielded his face with his hands.

Kay caught sight of Eagle at the entrance, carrying more stones. Now she understood his plan. "Just like the basketball toss at the carnival," she whispered. She hoped that he had learned something from Jack.

Eagle heaved another stone at the water. This one splashed down into the small pool and sent a wave cascading over its lip. Water splattered into the cauldron below. Steam and hot metal shards exploded.

"Stop!" Kay pleaded. "It's not working." A shard flew right at her, nicking her arm. "Ow! I just got hit."

"I just need one more stone in the right place!" Eagle screamed. "Just stay down." He reached for his last one. "I can do it."

Kay and AJ huddled.

Thick steam now obscured Eagle's vision. He would have to rely on his memory. Bending his knees and holding the stone at his waist, he flung it forward. It soared and landed with a *thud* right under the streaming water. The flow was instantly diverted, and the *crackling* ceased.

Relieved, Kay and AJ slowly emerged from behind the boulder. "Thanks, Eagle. That was quick thinking. I guess we all need to thank Jack when we get out of here. That was way better than a stuffed animal." She smiled and helped AJ up.

Eagle nodded proudly. "How's your arm?"

"It's okay." Kay inspected the small scrape.

"Yeah, thanks." AJ brushed off his shirt and pants. "You totally saved us." He tapped Eagle on his shoulder. "There's only one problem. We're still trapped."

The room was now full of dense fog. It was like a steam

bath. AJ focused on the water flowing into the crack in the floor. Steam poured out as more water flowed in.

"We've got to get out of here." AJ exhaled hard. "What can we do?" He glanced around nervously and felt the smooth walls. "What can we do?" he repeated.

"Maybe the water will cool this place down." Kay tried to be optimistic.

"No," AJ disagreed sternly. "It's really hot under there"—he pointed at the floor crack—"and all that water is going to become steam, with tons of pressure. Once the pressure gets too high, it will explode. It'll be like a super-heated geyser."

"A geyser! In here?" Kay exclaimed. "When? Soon?" Kay knew he was serious. "What's the plan?" She moved in closer. "You have a plan. Right?"

AJ thought hard, then stared intently at Kay. "What do you need to climb these walls?"

"Climbing gear," she said flatly. "Remember, we don't have any."

"How about if you had some spikes? Y'know, to hammer into the wall?" He kicked one of the metal shards littering the floor. "Can you use something like this?"

She studied the metal. "They would need to be longer—at least four inches." Kay surveyed the distance to the airshaft that was letting in light. "I'd need three. We could probably shimmy up from there."

"Then let's find them," AJ commanded. "Search the ground!"

The three friends fanned out to find spikes of the right size. It was hard to see through the steam. The temperature was rising fast, and more water was flowing down into the floor crack. The hissing got louder and bounced off the walls.

"That sounds really bad." Eagle frantically looked for more spikes, but dense fog surrounded them. They were drenched in sweat. They continued to search, tossing aside rocks and bits of metal.

"They're all too small." Kay scanned the room. Her voice cracked with worry. Eagle too, grew concerned. Then Kay spied a stone the size of a brick. "I can use this as a hammer." She sprang over to AJ. She panted, desperate for air. "But we still need spikes."

The room had become a furnace. They could hardly see each other through the thickening steam.

"I got one—no, two!" AJ shouted. He collected two spikes that were the right size, but they needed at least one more. He searched desperately for the last one. Then his eyes lit up. Without saying anything he moved to the cauldron. There was still some molten metal lining its bottom. He kicked it, knocking it onto its side. The metal poured onto the chamber floor and started to solidify—into a six-inch shard. It looked like a silver icicle. AJ kicked it with his sneakers into the water; it hissed as it cooled. After a few seconds he handed it to Kay.

"Here." He trembled. "Go to work!"

⊛ CHAPTER 5 ⊛

Kay stood directly below the crack from which the water flowed over the ledge. She reached up as high as her tall frame would permit. She scoured the rock, searching for the slightest indentation in the smooth walls. "There's one," she announced. Balancing carefully, she held the point of the spike against the small depression. She whacked the blunt end of the spike with her stone. The tip stuck, and she whacked it again, securing it in place. With great agility, Kay grabbed the spike and shimmied up by wedging her toe onto a tiny ledge. She swung her free foot up to share the spike with her hand. She carefully balanced on the spike and stood, with her open hands gripping the wall. Once she had steadied herself, she reached up as high as she could and whacked another spike into place. She now moved her free foot up to another tiny ledge midway between the two spikes. Climbing like a gymnast from rung to rung, balancing on the thinnest of edges, she positioned herself and secured the last and largest spike. She grabbed it with both hands to test it, and then scampered down to Eagle and AJ.

"There's no way I can climb on those spikes." AJ paced, waving the fog away from his face. "I can't do it."

"I don't think I can do it, either." Eagle lowered his head.

"Guys. Stop!" Kay was stern. "We're making a ladder—a human ladder—like ants do over water. AJ, you'll take the bottom section. Eagle will climb on you to get to the second spike. I'll be hanging from the third. Then AJ"— she pointed— "you'll climb over us both to get to the airshaft. Then, Eagle, you'll climb over me, and AJ will help you up. I'll follow. Got it?"

AJ and Eagle were stunned by the simplicity of Kay's plan.

"We're getting out of here," AJ announced triumphantly. He could hear the water bubbling below the floor. He knew that they only had a few more minutes before the geyser blew.

Kay quickly sprang up to the third spike and hung from it. "Let's go, AJ. You're up."

AJ cinched the straps of his backpack, grimacing as he felt the stones inside weighing him down. Nevertheless, with a running start, he jumped up and hung from the first spike. Eagle scrambled up over AJ as planned. He stood on AJ's shoulders, then reached up to grab the second spike. His outstretched hands clung to Kay's feet above.

"Okay, AJ," Kay shouted. "Climb up!"

AJ grabbed Eagle's legs and climbed up to his shoulders.

"Hey, that's my face!" Eagle grunted.

"Sorry." AJ pulled his foot back. He climbed over Kay

and into the airshaft above her. It was steep and narrow. He pressed his feet and forearms into the rock walls to support his weight. He shimmied upward and waited for the others. Eagle followed, climbing over Kay and into the opening. With AJ and Eagle now in the airshaft, it was Kay's turn to climb up. Eagle extended his hand to her while AJ grabbed Eagle's waist. She clasped Eagle's hand and pulled herself up to join her friends. They had successfully leapfrogged over one another into the tight space.

The airshaft cut into the rock at a steep angle. The sides were smooth, and the friends had to press their feet and forearms outward on opposite walls to keep from sliding backward.

"It's called 'stemming.'" Kay checked the position of her legs and feet. "Just push off and move up the shaft. Move your hands up and make sure you push out hard so you don't slip."

"I'm scared." AJ's voice cracked. "What if I get stuck?" His heavy backpack was hindering his progress. "Or fall?"

Eagle took a deep breath. "Just keep moving. You have enough room. Go toward the light." AJ pushed upward.

"That's right," Kay called up. "We're almost there. Keep going."

The three shimmied forward. They squeezed through the cramped shaft, which was like part of a ventilation system of a building. AJ noticed that the sidewalls shook as the pressure mounted under the chamber floor.

"Kay. Do you feel the vibrations?" AJ called back. Sweat poured off his face.

Kay twisted to look down. A thick plume of steam rose from the crack in the floor. Her eyes grew wide with fear.

"Move it! Now!" She pushed Eagle from behind.

The eruption of searing steam was seconds away.

"Keep moving!" Kay yelled. She was shaking.

"We're almost out!" AJ exclaimed. "We're almost out!" He moved his arms and legs as fast as he could.

The shaft shook. A high-pitched whistle rang out. Then came a deafening roar. The geyser erupted. The steam was filling the shaft right behind them.

AJ burst into the open air at the top of the outcropping, the same one they had entered from below. Eagle lunged next to him, then Kay.

"Jump!" she screamed, pushing them both toward some sagebrush on a ledge a few yards below.

"*Ahhhh!*" they yelled as they flew through the air. They landed with a *thud*, scraping their arms and legs on loose gravel and sharp sagebrush branches. Scorching steam was shooting out of the airshaft above with an earsplitting roar.

They lay motionless on their backs, watching the pressurized steam billow toward the sky. Water vapor rained down off to the side.

"That was way too close." Kay exhaled deeply. She held her bleeding arm.

"You think!" Eagle dusted himself off.

AJ got to his knees and smiled with relief. His face was covered in dirt. "This has been one long day."

⊛ CHAPTER 6 ⊛

"**W**hat time did he say he would meet us?" Jack checked his phone. "I'm starving."

"Eight," Kay replied. "Eagle's always a little late."

"And where's AJ? He's late, too." Jack grabbed a doughnut-like *churro* from the basket in the center of the table. "You told them the right time?" Jack's stomach growled.

"Just relax." Kay rolled her eyes. "Here, eat another *churro*." She pushed the basket over.

Just then Eagle and AJ showed up. Kay motioned them over.

The four friends were meeting for breakfast at *El Chico Loco*, Kay and Jack's father's other restaurant. *El Chico Loco* was just up the road from Fiery Bill's. This restaurant was in a small Mexican-style pueblo that had outdoor seating, and it served amazing food in huge portions. The breakfast special was the *huevos rancheros*. Jack was counting down the minutes until he could taste the eggs, refried beans, and tortillas.

Eagle's flip-flops slapped as he walked in. He carried a backpack. "Am I late?"

"Just a little," Kay smiled. "Jack was just about to eat his shoe."

He sat down. "Hey, I'm sorry. Thanks for waiting. I couldn't catch up with my grandfather yesterday, so I met him at the hot springs this morning. All his friends were there, and I couldn't break away. He gets up at the crack of dawn for that stuff. You know how he loves it. Then I saw something while I was heading over here. It took a little while for me to get it." Eagle patted his backpack.

Jack nodded. "It's no problem. We know how Talon loves the hot springs." He looked at Eagle's backpack. "What's in there?"

Eagle winked at Kay and AJ. "Nothing, really. Just something that was lying by the road. I'm bringing it back for my grandfather." He had a mischievous smile.

"Seriously, Eagle, what's in the pack?" Jack stood up and reached across the table to grab it. Eagle pulled it away quickly.

"Jack. I don't think you'll like it. Trust me." Eagle picked up a menu. "Let's get some food. I'm starving."

"Ummm." Jack huffed and sat back down. "Anyway, Kay tells me you guys had some adventure yesterday after you left the restaurant. I hear you almost got cooked!" Jack laughed. "Just kidding—I'm glad no one got hurt."

"Yeah, that was pretty scary," Eagle said. "But that place was amazing." He looked at Kay. "The molten metal and all that heat. We made a human ladder to get out. I even used the basketball throwing trick."

"I know. Kay told me." He put his long arm around her shoulders. "She's always getting us into trouble. Right?"

"Hey, I didn't cause the cave-in." Kay rolled her eyes.

"I know, I know," Jack nodded.

AJ unzipped his backpack and pulled out the hollow stones from the mine. "I took these." He showed Jack. "I'm not sure what they are. There was another one of these things in there, but bigger. I couldn't carry them both." AJ ran his hands over the carved-out centers, feeling the bumps and grooves.

Jack inspected the stones briefly. "They're heavy." He handed them back to AJ. "You're telling me." AJ placed them in his pack.

The waitress came over to take their order. "Where have you been hiding, Jack? I haven't seen you in a couple weeks."

"I've been helping my dad at Fiery Bill's. Believe me, I've been craving the *huevos rancheros* big time." Jack handed her the menus. "We'll go with four."

"How about you, Kay?" The waitress smiled. "What are you getting?"

There was a slight pause, and they all laughed.

"Very funny." Jack blushed. "I probably could eat four, but not today."

They agreed with the order, so the waitress closed her pad and walked away.

"So did Talon have any ideas about what we found yesterday?" AJ asked.

Eagle nodded and reached for a *churro*. "I didn't tell him

that we almost got cooked. But I did show him the picture Kay had taken of the mural in the mine. He recognized it immediately. He said it was from the Tectonic people."

"How does he know that?" AJ asked.

"Talon said the mural shows the mesa outside of town. Look—the flat-top mountain with those ruins of ancient buildings on it." Eagle zoomed in on the image on Kay's phone. "And the spiky peaks in the back—those are the rock spires and Mount Fuego. He's told me lots of stories about The Spires."

"Who are the Tectonic?" Jack asked, trying to catch up.

"They were a tribe that settled around here probably a thousand years ago." Eagle bit into the *churro*. The sugary fried dough spread over his tongue. He paused to savor it before continuing. "My grandfather told me to check out the mesa. He said the ancient ruins up there are pretty cool."

Just then the food arrived: four hot plates of eggs, refried beans, and tortillas. As Jack ate, he stared at Eagle's backpack. The friends were quiet as they enjoyed their food in the warm sun on the patio.

Kay broke the silence. "I think I've heard a legend about the Tectonic, but I can't remember how it went. AJ, do you know anything about them?"

AJ looked up from his plate. "Not too much. Just that they worshipped the Earth. Y'know, its power."

"Yep." Eagle nodded. "Talon said their culture was based on knowing the forces of the Earth. Kay, there is some ancient legend—'The Song of the Mountain.'"

"'Song of the Mountain'?" Jack perked up. "Sounds dramatic."

"That's right," Eagle continued. "There's an old story that the Tectonic could unlock some great power by playing a special song up by The Spires near Mount Fuego. The song filled the whole valley and was so powerful that it could start rockslides and change the whole landscape."

"Kay, you have that same effect when you sing in the shower," Jack joked. "All the dishes in the house shake."

"Very funny, Jack. So what happened to the Tectonic anyway?" Kay asked.

"Their culture was wiped out when the Spanish conquistadors came through here," Eagle said. "Talon told me the only thing that's left is the ruins at the mesa. He's told me stories about secret chambers up there, hidden like Egyptian tombs—though no one's ever found anything like that." He pushed his seat back and stood up. "But you know how sketchy these old stories are. That's why we should check the mesa out for ourselves."

"Let's go there after we finish up here." Kay checked the map on her phone. "It's not too far. We could bike."

"Sounds good," AJ agreed.

"Hey, I'm going to wash my hands real quick before we go." Eagle moved toward the restrooms. When he turned the corner, he stopped to glance back at the table. He knew Jack wouldn't be able to resist looking into his backpack while he was away. Sure enough, Jack was reaching for the pack.

"I don't think you should look in there, Jack," Kay protested. "He warned you."

"Yeah, whatever," Jack replied. He positioned the backpack next to him on the bench. "Well, let's just take a quick peek and see what he's hiding."

Jack loosened the cord and opened the flap. He couldn't see anything, so he stood and held the backpack up to his eyes.

"Careful," AJ warned.

Jack moved into the light. Then the pack's contents came into focus. "*Ahhhh!*" he screamed. He dropped the pack and stumbled back into Kay's lap. "He's got a snake in there!" he shouted. "A live snake!" He shuddered.

"He told you not to look in there," Kay laughed, pushing him away.

Eagle ran over. He had watched from across the patio. "Did I forget to mention I found a desert king snake on my ride over here? My bad!" He broke down in laughter. "You should like this one, Jack. They eat rattlers, but they're harmless to us." Eagle collected his backpack, making sure the snake was still inside. He cinched the top tight and shot a smile over to Jack. "That's payback for the 'heart attack' you gave me with the sauce."

Kay giggled, trying to contain herself. "He did warn you. You looked in there all on your own." She continued to laugh.

"I know. I know." Jack got to his feet and dusted off his clothes. He smiled. "Nice one, Eagle. Very nice—But it's so on."

⬙ CHAPTER 7 ⬙

"**C**heck out that view!" Kay marveled. "AJ, get up here. You can see all the way to the rock spires and the volcano of Mount Fuego."

"I'm coming." AJ gasped. He scrambled over a few more rocks and pulled himself up next to Kay, Eagle, and Jack. "Wow, you're right." He took another deep breath. "Incredible."

The four friends had arrived on top of the mesa. Scattered over the flat field were the ruins of stone buildings. Below, the El Gato River sliced through a plain dotted with sagebrush on its way toward town.

"How come nobody else is up here?" AJ wondered.

"It's a historical site of a Native tribe," Eagle replied. "Most people don't care about that stuff. Works for us: we get the place all to ourselves."

The friends walked over to a plaque. AJ read the text aloud:

The structures at this site were erected by the Tectonic people in approximately 1400 AD. This tribe was unusual in its advanced knowledge of metal work, geology, and physical sciences. Yet they also dealt in religion. Legend has it that they held rituals at The Spires, a rock formation visible from this mesa, that created songs of such power that they could reshape the land. The tribe vanished shortly after the Spanish conquest in 1537.

"Rituals at The Spires?" Kay scoffed. "What'd they do? Parachute onto them?"

"Kay, what do you mean?" AJ asked.

"Oh, don't get her started." Jack shook his head. "She's been wanting to get up to those things for years. I've never seen her do so much research."

"That's true," Kay nodded. "AJ, do you have your binoculars with you?"

"Right here," he replied.

"Let me show you." Kay directed everyone to the edge of the mesa. "There." She pointed. "Take a look."

AJ viewed The Spires through his binoculars.

"Do you see all those columns of sheer rock?" Kay asked. "They're all stacked together. Each one hundreds of feet tall."

"And you want to climb them?" Eagle asked, puzzled.

"You bet," Kay said. "The view of the volcano from there has got to be amazing. But there's no trail."

Jack chimed in. "And believe me, guys, she's looked. She's studied all the maps. It's really isolated."

"That's right," Kay nodded.

"Well, like the sign says"—Eagle put his arm around Kay—"it's an ancient legend."

"Hey." Jack gathered everyone together. "Let's check out the ruins. See if we can find a secret chamber," he joked. He led the way over to one of the buildings. "I wonder what this was for?" Three sides were still standing, but one and the roof had collapsed.

"Nobody knows for sure," Eagle said, following close behind. "The Tectonic may have lived up here. But the place seems a little small for a full village. My grandfather thinks it could have been a shrine of some kind. These ruins here—the small buildings around this big one—it all looks just like the mural in the mine."

Kay pulled up the photo on her phone. "That's amazing! It really does."

Meanwhile, AJ had walked over to the central ruin. The sidewalls must have been ten feet tall; it towered over him. "What was this place?" he muttered. A few steps led down to a floor several feet below the mesa surface. He walked down. The floor was tiled with stone and extended ten feet from the base of the steps to a back wall. On it was a faded mural, six feet wide by three feet high, of the surrounding landscape. AJ could make out the rocky spires and Mount Fuego. A thin rim of rock framed the picture.

AJ scanned the walls above him. Many large stones had broken off; debris littered the tile floor. Stepping carefully, he went over to inspect the mural, but he tripped and fell. He looked back at the place where he had lost his balance. He saw Jack at the base of the steps. AJ was embarrassed. He got up and brushed himself off.

"You all right?" Jack called.

"Yep. Just scraped my knee."

Jack hopped off the last step and spied a ring of bricks around a hole in the center of the floor. They were obscured by the shadows cast by the surrounding walls. "You tripped on these."

Jack pulled out his phone and shone his light into the opening. AJ walked over. He knelt down, lost his balance again, and accidentally knocked into Jack. Startled by the sudden shove, Jack lost his grip on his phone. Swish—it fell into the hole.

"Are you kidding me?!" Jack shrieked.

"I'm sorry," AJ apologized. He was concerned that Jack was going to blow his top. "Did your phone really just fall in there?"

"It just slipped out." Jack frantically put his arm in the hole up to his elbow, trying to retrieve the lost phone. "I can't believe it," he muttered. "This is crazy." Jack fished around, reaching as far down as he could. His fingers made contact.

"Did you get it?" AJ hoped he had.

Jack wiggled his fingers and touched the side of the phone. "Phew. Got it." Jack exhaled. "That's a relief." He went to pull his arm out. Then panic gripped him. "Uh oh!"

"What?" AJ asked.

"My arm—it's stuck."

"Stuck?" AJ repeated in disbelief.

"Stuck. I can't get it out." Jack flexed his muscles. "I can't move it. Help me, AJ. Before Kay sees."

AJ moved in closer. "Wow. It's really in there. Hold on, I think I can help." AJ reached into his bag for sunscreen.

"I'm not going anywhere." Jack rolled his eyes.

"Try this." AJ squirted a big glob on the side of Jack's

arm. The cool cream slid down his skin and into the hole. "This stuff is pretty slippery. See if you can work it down in there."

Jack slowly moved his arm. "Ow. Something's scratching me. I hope it's not some poison bug." He grew concerned.

"Just pull out slowly," AJ cautioned.

Jack followed his instructions. To his relief, his arm started to slide. After a little more wiggling, his whole arm came out. "Man, that was close." He looked to see if Kay was watching.

"It's all red." AJ inspected it. "Does it hurt?"

Jack looked at the tiny red bumps on his forearm. They made a prickly pattern. "Only my pride." He wiped his arm off and stuck his phone deep in his pocket.

Moments later, Kay and Eagle showed up.

"What's up with your arm, Jack?" Kay asked as she approached. She noticed it immediately. "It's all red."

"His phone fell in that hole and he got stuck trying to get it." AJ answered for him.

"What?" Kay took a moment to process what he said. "You got stuck in that hole? Are you serious?" She laughed. "How's that possible?"

"Does it matter? Thanks for telling her, AJ." Jack turned bright red. "Let's move on."

"It's my fault," AJ admitted. "I bumped into him."

"Still," Kay smiled. "Since it's obvious you're okay, I can enjoy that it's kinda funny."

Eagle redirected the conversation. "Hey, this place is amazing." He studied the framed mural of the rocky spires and Mount Fuego on the back wall. "This is the only building that has these sunken steps and a mural. I wonder what they did up here?"

"Why would the Tectonic have a mural of this mesa in the mine? How are they connected? We should talk to Talon," AJ suggested.

"That's a great idea," Eagle agreed. "My grandfather loves to tell the old stories. And maybe he can tell us more about the secret chamber." Eagle scanned the tumbled down stone walls. "I don't see anything like that up here."

"Does he have a tale about how not to get your arm stuck in a hole at an ancient ruin?" Kay teased Jack.

"I thought we were moving on," Jack replied curtly.

"You're right," Kay said. "I'm sorry. But what are the odds. Right?"

Even Jack laughed.

AJ walked over to the framed mural on the back wall. He explored the surface with his hand. "I'm going to research the Tectonic and this place," AJ decided. "Try to figure out what they were all about."

"I'm sure you will, AJ," Jack laughed. "And you'll have a twenty-page paper finished by tomorrow to prove it."

⊛ CHAPTER 8 ⊛

*K*nock knock. Kay tapped on AJ's front door. "He must be downstairs," she thought. She let herself in and made her way down to the basement.

There, piles of tools and junk blocked the way. Every surface was covered with all sorts of stuff that AJ used to build or repair practically anything. He had collected them from yard sales and second-hand stores. He had a system for finding everything, but to anyone else, the place looked like a complete mess. But one item stood alone on a special table. It was his prize possession: his 3D printer. That wasn't from a yard sale. His mother had bought it for him last Christmas.

Kay spied him sitting on a couch in front of the TV. Papers were strewn everywhere. She walked over. "Did you sleep down here?"

"Come here, quick." AJ patted the spot next to him. "Oh, too late. You just missed it."

"Missed what?" Kay sat down. "What's up?"

"The news. Did you see the news?"

"Who watches the news?" she scoffed.

"They talked about the earthquakes." He paused and turned toward her. "Mount Fuego's going to explode. Everyone needs to evacuate."

"What?" Kay was shocked.

"Explode!" he repeated. "Well—maybe. It *may* explode. Pressure is building up underground. That's what's causing all the shaking." AJ talked fast. "The pressure is really high around Mount Fuego. They say that this has happened before—every five hundred years—like clockwork. And they've tracked eruptions going back thousands of years. They could tell that once a huge explosion blew off the mountaintop. That's why there's a giant crater up there. But the last time, a huge crack opened up on the mountain's north side facing away from town, and lava just flowed down into the far valley. You can still see the black volcanic rock all around there. It's from that ancient lava flow. The scientists couldn't explain why it would do one or the other."

"Does that matter?" Kay stood stunned. "Don't we all need to leave either way?"

"Well, if the lava just comes out the far side, it's pretty safe. If that happens, the pressure under the mountain gets lowered and there's no explosion. As long as you're not in the lava's path, it should be okay. But if the pressure gets too high—boom! The whole mountain goes up, and our town with it. We would definitely need to leave before that."

"Did they say when this will happen? Is there time?"

"Yes," he reassured her. "The pressure's building, but it's

not critical yet. They said they would know what's going to happen within a few months. There's still time," he repeated.

Kay let out a sigh of relief. "A few months." She sat motionless. Her thoughts raced about the possible destruction of the town: Her house. Their school. Her dad's restaurants. Everything.

AJ left the couch and walked over to stacks of paper on his desk. He flipped though his research materials. He pulled out an article and handed it to her. "Like I said, something happened five hundred years ago—Mount Fuego didn't explode. Lava flowed out harmlessly, and that lowered the pressure. Look."

He handed Kay a photo of Mount Fuego's north slope covered in black volcanic rock. The hardened lava extended for miles. "What's weird is that I've been reading this stuff about the Tectonic, too, and their legends talk about how they could control the volcanic eruptions. Like the plaque up at the mesa said, they had some way to unleash great power and reshape the land. And Kay, you're going to love this"— AJ handed her an article—"the rock spires play a big role in the legend."

"The Spires?"

"Yes. Maybe they can somehow affect the lava flow? Who knows? It's all very confusing. We definitely need to talk with Talon. He might know something about all this."

"Talon? Great power? Spires?" Kay said. "AJ, you're nuts!" She shook her head. "What does Talon have to do with this? No one can get to The Spires. And that volcano's going to explode. Nobody can stop it!"

"We need to figure this out." AJ reached for his backpack

and the carved stones. "I need to show these to Talon. We found them in the Tectonic mine, right? And we saw the mural of the mesa in there, too. There's got to be a connection." AJ zipped up his pack. "Call Eagle and Jack. Let's meet up at the wind sculpture. Then we'll go find Talon and see what he has to say."

Kay grew annoyed. "What's to figure out, AJ? We need to leave our town. We all need to leave. Mount Fuego is going to explode."

AJ swung his heavy backpack over his shoulder. "Yes, that's probably true, but not tomorrow. Just call them."

✸ CHAPTER 9 ✸

Kay, AJ, and Jack were at the base of the wind sculpture in the town square, waiting for Eagle to arrive. People were milling about at the farmers' market, buying fresh produce. Everyone seemed surprisingly calm, even though by now they all had heard the news. Fliers posted everywhere announced a town meeting in two days at which the mayor would give updates.

"What is this thing anyway?" Jack asked. He looked up at the wind sculpture, which flashed as it spun. It was spiral shaped with metal rods attached to a central pole. Reflective clay pieces were attached to the ends of each rod. The pieces appeared to move up and down as it spun. "I've passed by this thing like a million times, but I don't know anything about it."

"Look at the sign," AJ said. "'The artist found these clay fragments in the river.' The glaze makes them sparkle. Pretty cool, huh?"

"Yeah, love the sparkles," Kay said. "There must be bits of metal in there. Remember, Jack, we could see it from Devil's Drop?"

"Oh, yeah," Jack nodded. He turned back to watch the crowd. "I can't believe we might all have to leave. It's so amazing." Jack paused for a few seconds, then looked at AJ. "What are we doing here? I'm getting hungry."

"That's a shock!" AJ scoffed. "We're waiting for Eagle, and then we're going to see Talon. I need to show him the stuff we found in the mine." He patted his backpack. "If you're hungry, hit that burrito stand right there. Go grab something for all of us."

"Sounds good." Jack walked over. Moments later, Eagle arrived.

"Hey guys," Eagle said. "Can you believe the news? We have to evacuate—the volcano's going to explode."

"Maybe," AJ said. "They said it might explode. It didn't the last time. The pressure's not high enough yet. If it goes down, we'll be okay."

"That's a big *if*," Eagle observed.

"It is," AJ agreed. "But some of the stories I've read—about the Tectonic—they actually talk about stopping the eruptions of Mount Fuego. I'm hoping Talon can shed some light. Do you know where he is?"

"Where else would he be at this time?" Eagle smiled. "He's at the hot springs with his friends. He told me the water temperature has really heated up, probably from all the earthquakes, so they're siphoning off some river water to cool the pools down."

"Lead the way," AJ motioned.

"We need to wait for Jack," Kay said. "Here he comes. Let's eat here and then go."

The friends ate their burritos while watching the crowd and listening to the hum of the wind sculpture turning above them. The oddly-shaped pieces twisted in a spiral pattern. Even faint currents of air made the sculpture spin.

After they had finished their burritos, they grabbed their bikes and rode off to meet Talon. The friends didn't talk much. They all were preoccupied, thinking how an eruption would affect them and the town.

Their ride out to the hot springs led them down a dirt road that wound through a canyon. Their bicycle wheels crunched on scattered gravel. Sagebrush lined the route. Eagle, out front, suddenly veered and braked. The others pulled up alongside.

"What's up?" Kay called.

Eagle dismounted, knelt, and gazed down the length of the road. His put his hand to his forehead, shielding his eyes from the sun's glare. Kay knelt next to him.

"What's up?" she asked again.

Eagle pointed with his other hand. "Looks like they're all crossing the road."

"What's crossing the road?" Jack squinted.

Eagle walked a few steps, zeroing in on a few fist-sized objects moving on the gravel. He bent over and pointed. "That!"

Jack got off his bike and walked over. He looked down. His eyes grew wide. He jumped back. "That's a tarantula! There're hundreds of them! All over the place." He shivered and stumbled toward his bike.

"It's okay, Jack." AJ went over to inspect the insects. "They're just crossing the road. Y'know, you've lived here for years. You'd think by now you'd get used to these things."

"Are you kidding?! They're disgusting! And creepy."

Eagle grabbed a stick. "Here, check it out." He picked up a tarantula and waved it at Jack.

"Get that thing away from me!" Jack protested.

"How can a big guy like you be so scared of a little insect?" Kay laughed.

"Little? Yeah, yeah. It's so funny," Jack mocked. "Now let's go. Are we going to meet Talon or what?" He got back on his bike and pedaled cautiously. He wove in and out among the spiders, making sure he didn't run over any of them. When he saw a clearing, he hightailed it through. His friends followed close behind.

They continued down the canyon. When they reached the river, they dismounted and stowed their bike at the trailhead. They followed the trail up a ridge, and from the top, they could see Talon and his friends below working to redirect the cool river water into a shallow canal they had dug. The trail banked to the right, skirting an open field of hardened mud pocked with holes.

"It looks like Swiss cheese," Kay noted. She read a small hand-written sign posted in front. "*Muddy area. Keep out!*"

"Muddy?" Jack scoffed. "It looks about as hard as dirt can get." He threw a rock, which bounced on the surface. "Come on, guys. Let's go through it. It's a shortcut."

"Let's stay on the trail, Jack," AJ replied. "It goes around the edge. It's not too much longer."

"It's a lot longer, but whatever," Jack relented. "Maybe

it's muddy when it rains," he muttered.

After a few more minutes on the trail, Eagle spied Talon as he turned the corner. Talon was working hard at digging a trench. His strong hands gripped the shovel as sweat poured off his wrinkled face. When he caught sight of Eagle and the others, he stopped shoveling and pulled back his long grey hair. He called to Eagle, "Hey, you guys here for a dip?"

"Not today," Eagle smiled.

"Hey, Talon." AJ waved as he approached. "You're working on some big project here."

"Yeah. The spring is really hot. We joked about bringing some hotdogs to throw in and cook."

"That sounds good," Jack smiled. "I love hot dogs."

"You just ate." Kay shook her head.

"Crazy news about the earthquakes and volcano, huh?" Talon said.

"You don't seem too concerned," Eagle observed.

"Well," he paused, "not yet. I suspect that's why you're here. Right, AJ?" Talon said with a knowing glint, focusing on AJ. "Come on, let's talk over here." He motioned everyone to sit on the boulders that bordered the hot spring.

"Eagle told me that you all found an old Tectonic mine the other day and so you want more information about them." Talon talked slowly. "The Tectonic were a mysterious people—very advanced. They could even forge metal tools. Did you see anything like that in the mine?"

AJ reached into his backpack. He pulled out the two carved stones and handed them to Talon. "We found these. They're not metal."

"These don't look like tools." Talon was puzzled.

"The whole place was like a furnace," Kay said. "And there was metal. A whole pot of it! Bubbling over a fire pit. But there wasn't much else. Just those carved rocks and the mural of the mesa."

Talon studied the halves closely. He ran his hands over the bumps on the inner surfaces. He held the stones up to the light.

AJ continued. "There was another one of these stones in there, but we didn't have a lot of time." He shot Kay and Eagle a quick look, not wanting to give too many details of their narrow escape. "And it was a lot heavier. This was the only one I could carry out. Do you know what it is?"

"These bumps are interesting. I wonder if it's a tool of some kind." Talon studied it closely, then handed the stones back to AJ. "Do you all know the legends of the Tectonic?"

"Just what we read at the mesa," Kay said.

"I did some research, too," AJ added. "But we were hoping you could give us more details."

Talon reclined on a smooth rock. He prepared to tell the stories.

The friends moved in closer.

"What I know of them is what my father told me, which is what his father told him. We've tried to keep alive the ancient stories, even though we are not direct descendants." He paused to take a sip of water. "The Tectonic knew that Mount Fuego was an active volcano and would explode at regular intervals. Legend has it that the tribe had figured out a way to reach the rock spires on the near side of the crater and unleash such a powerful force that they could reshape the land and somehow control the eruptions."

"The sign at the mesa talked about 'The Song of the Mountain,'" AJ said. "How does that fit in?"

"According to their stories, the song unleashed that great power." Talon looked at their skeptical faces. "I know it seems unlikely that a song can unleash any power, much less a great one, but maybe the song is really a ritual they performed. It's hard to say." He paused and looked at AJ. "As I'm sure you've read, the Tectonic had studied the Earth. They understood that an eruption is the result of a build-up of pressure. If they could release some of it—in a controlled way—it would prevent the mountain from exploding."

"Kind of like if you shake a soda bottle and open it quickly," Kay said, "it'll spray all over you. But if you open it slowly to let out the gas, it doesn't spray."

"Right," Talon smiled.

"So how do we find out more about The Song of the Mountain?" Eagle asked.

Talon studied all their faces. "There's no easy way to know for certain. But the legend also says that the mesa holds the clues. My father believed that there is a secret chamber buried deep within the mesa. In it, the elders hid their knowledge of the passageway to The Spires and the ritual they performed there."

"If it was so important to help save them from destruction, why would they hide it?" Jack asked.

"Too much power," Talon said flatly. "Only the elders could be trusted to use it wisely."

"Of course it's a secret." Jack rolled his eyes.

"Nothing's easy, Jack," Talon said. "Unfortunately, the Tectonic died off quickly, mostly from disease when the

Spanish explorers came through five hundred years ago. There are no direct descendants around to ask. Their secrets died with them."

"So no one's found a secret chamber up on the mesa?" Kay asked.

Talon shook his head. "No. I've scoured that place a million times, looking for some clue. If there's something up there, it's locked away pretty tight."

"Speaking of tight, Jack got his arm stuck in a hole up there," Kay said. "Right at the base of the stairs of the biggest building. You can still see the red marks on his arm."

"Hey, my phone fell in. I had to get it," Jack explained. He held his arm up for Talon to see.

"Yeah, I know that hole. I've always wondered what that was. But I never stuck my arm in it." He shot Jack a stern glare. "There could be spiders in there," he chided him.

"Spiders?" Jack shivered. "I didn't think of that."

Talon inspected the marks on Jack's arm. "That's an interesting pattern." He paused. "Hope that doesn't hurt too much. You should be more careful." He grew thoughtful.

"Do you believe the legend?" AJ asked. "It seems pretty out there."

Talon spoke softly. "The legend was passed down from generation to generation, so lots can be exaggerated over time. What's clear is that there was no explosion as usual five hundred years ago, just the big lava flow on the north side. Even today, scientists don't understand why or how that happened. I believe there is some truth to it all," Talon added forcefully. "Finding the secret chamber would go a long way toward knowing for sure." Talon pointed to the carved stones in AJ's hand. "See if you can figure out what those things are. I've never seen anything quite like them. I think it's a key to help unlock the mystery."

With that, Talon got up and walked away to rejoin his friends. He seemed perfectly at ease, as if, despite the predicted evacuation and explosion, he didn't have a care in the world. He looked back. "I'll see you later tonight, Eagle."

"I guess that's our cue to go," Eagle said. "Did he help us, AJ?"

"Maybe." AJ looked at the stones. "He did say that these are key. Key to what, I don't know." He put them in his pack.

They walked back on the path out of the canyon, thinking about what Talon had told them. Soon they reached the expanse of hard mud.

"I'm not walking all the way around this time," Jack announced. "I'm going for the shortcut." He knelt and tapped the ground. "It's solid. It hasn't rained. I'm doing it."

"You can do what you want, Jack, but I'm taking the trail," Kay said. She headed off.

"Me, too." AJ followed Kay. "Why don't we race around? See who gets to the bikes first."

"You're on." Eagle high-fived Jack. "It looks solid, and we're definitely going to beat you."

Jack stepped onto the dry mud field. "Let's do it." They raced off, making a beeline for the other side.

"Let's go, AJ." Kay bolted along the trail. "There's no way I'm letting them beat us."

AJ took off, following Kay. They raced around the mud field, glancing over to check on Jack and Eagle's progress. AJ and Kay had a lot more ground to cover.

Jack clomped over the shortcut, his long strides pounding over the pocked ground. It crunched as he ran. His feet made shallow imprints, reminding him of running on hardened snow. Eagle followed cautiously, as if he were crossing a minefield, avoiding the deep pockmarks and sticking to Jack's path. The crunching got louder as they ventured further over the hardened crust. Then Jack abruptly motioned for Eagle to stop.

"I don't think this stuff is stable." Jack scanned the mud in front of him. They were almost at the other side.

"That's probably why that sign's there," Eagle said. Mild dread washed over him.

Jack was only a few yards from hooking back up to the trail. Then he heard cracking.

"Oh no," he gasped. "It's breaking." The hardened crust was too thin to hold him up. Mud bubbled up around his feet.

"Eagle, go back," Jack called.

Eagle turned. He saw Kay and AJ on the trail about halfway around. Then he looked back toward Jack. "Oh, no," Jack groaned. He sank in knee-deep.

Eagle saw Jack lose his balance and tumble face down into the mud. He floundered to one side. Trying desperately to rise, he slipped again. Eagle lunged to help him, but he too fell in mud, but only up to his knees.

"Are you guys okay?" Kay had seen Jack fall like a tree. He was now sitting up and floundering around, feeling for solid ground. He was covered in mud.

Eagle sloshed around, trying to right himself. "Sort of," he grunted, struggling to free his legs. "It's not very deep, but I think I just lost my shoe. It's like a vacuum in here. Too much suction." He reached down into the mud to feel for his lost flip-flop.

"Well, this is a sight," AJ laughed. He was now only a few yards from Jack. "Looks a little muddy," he observed with a wry smile.

"It's not funny," Jack scolded. He tried to steady himself on his knees.

"Well, it's sorta funny," Eagle admitted. "We probably should have stayed on the trail. But, it *is* warm and squishy in here." He reached deeper into the thick mud. "Hey, I think I just found my flip-flop." He felt something firm. "I hope it's my flip-flop." He flashed a worried look, then exhaled. He pulled it out, but the pop of its release knocked him down. After struggling for a minute, he leaned back, relaxing in the warm mud bath. "My aunt pays big bucks for this at a spa. It's supposed to be good for the skin."

"I'm not at a spa," Jack said bluntly. "I'm super dirty." At last Jack peeled himself up. He saw an imprint of his face in the mud. "Hey, AJ. Check this out. It's a perfect mold." Jack admired it. "Looks good, right?"

AJ peered at the imprint from the safety of the trail. A thought popped into his head.

"AJ. I've seen that look before," Kay said. "What's up?" She hurried over.

AJ retrieved one of the carved-out stones from his pack. He knelt down next to the muddy surface and pressed the stone—carved side down—into the mud. He then gently lifted it out and smiled as the imprint came into view. "I know what this is!" he exclaimed. "It's just like Talon said." He held up the stone triumphantly. "This is the key!"

⚛ CHAPTER 10 ⚛

Eagle and Jack had made their way out of the mud. They were sitting on rocks at the field's edge, scraping dirt off their clothes and bodies. Once Eagle had cleaned himself off, AJ handed him the carved stones.

"So this is a mold to make a key?" Eagle held the halves together, revealing a small hole on the top.

"Yes. I have a hunch that the key just might fit into that hole on top of the mesa. The bumps there, the ones that left marks on Jack's arm, make the same pattern that's on the inside of these stones." AJ held the open half of the stone up against Jack's arm. "See? The reds dots line up."

"Good thing I dropped my phone," Jack chuckled.

"So how do we do it? " Eagle asked. "Do we just pour some kind of molten metal in here till it hardens?"

"That's my guess." AJ nodded.

"Do you really think this key will unlock something up

there?" Kay asked.

"There's only one way to find out—we need to make it and try it," AJ said.

"That's great." Jack shook his head. "But how do we do that? I don't happen to have any molten metal lying around."

"I have a friend who works in a machine shop," AJ said. "He's helped me make stuff before. The only thing is, he can't do it when his boss is around. He almost got fired last time he helped me."

"So he can do it, but we just need to get his boss out of the way?" Kay asked.

"That's right," AJ confirmed.

"Jack, do you have any ideas?" Kay smiled. "You're good at this type of stuff."

Jack wiped more mud from his face. "Who's his boss?"

"Mr. Fish," AJ replied.

"I know him." As the friends walked over to their bikes, Jack's mind raced, thinking of a plan. "He's the big guy who eats at Fiery Bill's every Wednesday. Man, that guy can eat—maybe even more than me." Jack was impressed.

"Yeah, that's him," AJ said.

"Do you think you can do something?" Eagle straddled his bike. "Can you keep him occupied while AJ's friend makes the metal key?"

"I think I can." Jack had a devilish smile. "But I'm going to need your help, Eagle. You in?"

"Sure," he nodded.

"Great! We'll make it work," Jack said.

With that, the friends got on their bikes and rode back to town.

⟐ CHAPTER 11 ⟐

"**W**hy me?" Eagle protested. "You're the one with the big appetite."

"Because I work there," Jack replied. "I can't be in a chicken wing eating contest at a restaurant my father owns. The prize will be four free meals. I get that anyway. Besides, Dad loves the idea. He says it will bring in more business."

"But what about Kay? Can't she do it?"

"Hey, AJ and I won the race around the mud." She laughed. "Plus, like Jack said, our dad owns the place."

"Fine." Eagle relented. "So what do I need to do?"

"You just have to eat as many chicken wings as Mr. Fish. You don't have to win. We just need to keep him at the restaurant while Kay and AJ get the key made."

Eagle looked nervous. "Mr. Fish is huge! I can't keep up with him."

"We just need to slow him down." Jack put his arm

around Eagle. "I'll help. I'll stretch out the event. You'll see. We'll need about an hour and a half, right?" He looked at AJ.

"Yes, that should do it," AJ confirmed. "My friend will have it all set up before we get there."

"You'll be okay, Eagle," Kay encouraged him. "You've got to take this one for the team."

Eagle slumped. "Fine."

"We'll make fliers, and I'll make sure the Big Fish gets one," Jack said. "He wouldn't miss this. It's going to be fun."

* * * * * *

A few days later, they were ready for the eating contest. Jack had done a great job of promoting the event; a line of people extended out the door. Five dollars entitled the contestants to an all-you-can-eat BBQ wing experience.

Fiery Bill's had a carnival-like atmosphere that day. Each table had a huge mound of BBQ wings at its center. They were spiced but not sauced. The participants had to take a wing, dip it in sauce, eat it, and then discard the bones. Water pitchers ringed each table in anticipation of the contestants' needs.

Spectators gathered around the tables as the participants walked in, primed like boxers at a match. Twelve people had signed up, but just as Jack and his father had hoped, they had brought friends. The wait staff was busy serving as the main attraction drew near.

"Is that him?" Eagle shuddered.

The Big Fish lumbered onto the patio, smiling and talking to his friends. He was six-foot-four and weighed close to three hundred pounds. He had a scruffy beard and looked like a football lineman. Even though Eagle had an athletic build, he seemed puny by comparison.

Jack nodded. "Yep. He's got to be the favorite here." Jack scanned the crowd, then looked at his phone and read a text from Kay. She and AJ were already at the machine shop. "Just slow him down, Eagle. That's all you need to do. You got this—for the team. Right?"

Eagle wore an apprehensive smile.

Jack stood on a chair. He spoke to the crowd. "Welcome, everyone, to our first annual all-you-can-eat BBQ chicken wing eating contest."

Everyone cheered.

"Let's get it on!" a voice shouted. "My money's on The Big Fish." Mr. Fish stood, taking in the applause.

"Okay, okay." Jack stalled for time. He knew that Kay and AJ had entered the machine shop the moment Mr. Fish had left for lunch, so they must have been well on their way to making the key. He turned his attention back to the contest. "Here are the rules." He surveyed the crowd. "Whoever eats the most wings in the next twenty-five minutes wins four free meals here at Fiery Bill's. Pretty simple. We'll be using five different sauces, starting with mild and moving up to super hot." Jack gave Eagle an encouraging look. "I'll switch the sauces every five minutes. Everyone clear on the rules?"

The crowd settled in, eating their own food and watching the spectacle.

"Let's go, Fish!" his friends called.

Jack held his hands up. "Contestants, are you ready?" He paused dramatically. "Get set." He lowered his hands. "Go!"

Eagle sat directly across from Mr. Fish. Eagle watched

him gulp down three wings before he had finished even one. Eagle remembered that his friends were counting on him and picked up his pace. He wanted to eat as many as he could with the milder sauce so he wouldn't have to bear the pain of the hotter ones. He grabbed a wing, ate it, and grabbed another. Mr. Fish looked worried as Eagle moved into the lead.

After five minutes and the second sauce, the pace of eating slowed. The crowd cheered, and people meandered through the patio as they watched. Jack and Kay's father, Bill, worked the crowd, talking with the guests, making sure they all were having fun. The field of contestants thinned. Jack announced a change in the sauce.

"Now we're going with sauce number three: The 'Fireballer'!" Jack placed fresh squeeze-bottles on the tables.

Eagle pressed ahead. It was clear that Mr. Fish was no stranger to hot sauces. Mr. Fish shot Eagle a stern look as he squeezed the Fireballer onto his plate. Eagle now looked worried. Sweat streamed from his brow, and his mouth was already numb.

Jack's phone vibrated, signaling a text from Kay. He looked down and smiled.

"Wow! That's too hot for me." One of the contestants pushed her plate aside. "I'm out!" She reached for the milder sauce and kept eating. Her friends joined her and laughed.

"Now sauce number four: 'Devil's Breath'!" Jack yelled.

The change in hot sauce was taking its toll. One by one, all the contestants dropped out, leaving only Eagle and The Big Fish.

"Fish! Fish! Fish!" the crowd chanted. He had pulled ahead and wasn't slowing down. He looked over at Eagle, waiting for him to quit.

"It's not over yet, big guy," Eagle taunted him. He grabbed another wing. His stomach gurgled, and he clenched his fists to focus his strength. His mouth was completely on fire. He knew he trailed Mr. Fish by just a few pieces, and he wondered how much longer his friends would need. Mr. Fish seemed unfazed by the hot sauces and looked like he was just hitting his stride.

"Okay, guys—one last sauce." Jack pounded the table to get their attention. "It's time for the 'Heart Attack'!" He moved the bottles into position.

"Just stall him a little longer," Jack whispered in Eagle's ear. "You're doing great."

Overcoming his dread of experiencing the Heart Attack again, Eagle grabbed another wing. He dipped it in the sauce and then placed it in his mouth, avoiding his lips so they wouldn't burn. He bit down. Sweat streamed off his flushed face. His eyes watered, and he fumbled for water. Mr. Fish struggled, too. Eagle knew he had to compete just a little longer for his friends. He doused his mouth with ice, stalling for time. Then, through his watery eyes, he spied Kay and AJ. Was he dreaming? How could they be here already?

AJ flashed Eagle a thumb's-up. He then pointed to the inside of his backpack. Confused, Eagle turned to Jack.

"Oh, I forgot to tell you," Jack said dryly. "Kay texted me a while ago that they had finished. It took a lot less time than they thought it would. But you're doing great. Hope your mouth isn't too hot." Jack burst into laughter.

Eagle jumped up from his seat and started to chase after Jack. They both ran off. "I am gonna get you for this," Eagle shouted. Jack just kept running.

Mr. Fish pumped his fist in victory, and the crowd went wild. In Jack's absence, Bill stepped in and crowned The Big Fish as the champion.

⊛ CHAPTER 12 ⊛

"There's still no one here," Kay observed.

"Well, it's pretty late in the day, and like I said, most people don't care about these old ruins," Eagle said. "Besides, it makes it easier for us to do our thing. Right?"

Kay nodded. "AJ, are you coming or what?"

"I'm coming," he grunted. "For some reason, I'm the one carrying this metal key. It's heavy, y'know."

"Heavy?" Jack scoffed.

The friends were back at the mesa. When AJ finally reached the top, he walked over to the central ruin, the one with the steps leading down. The framed mural on the back wall reflected the late afternoon light.

Kay and Eagle were hovering over the hole at the base of the steps. Eagle was cleaning it out. He had brought some tools and brushes. AJ walked over and stood at Eagle's shoulder. He was excited to see if the cylinder key they had made would fit.

AJ nudged Eagle aside. "That should be good," he decided. "The sunscreen in there will lube it up. Right, Jack?"

"Yeah, just don't get your arm stuck," Kay teased.

Jack changed the subject. "You really think that metal thing is going to fit into there?"

"We'll know soon enough, right?" AJ held the cylinder over the hole. The key was around a foot long and six inches wide; the hole was just a little larger. Small spikes of various lengths and thicknesses stuck out all over the cylinder. AJ positioned it, lining up the bumps and ridges with the indentations in the hole. He pushed the key in, jiggling it left and right. It slid down until its top edge was a few inches above the ground. It locked in with a click. "It fits!" AJ exclaimed. Not sure which way to turn it, he tried going right. It didn't budge. Then he tried going left. Again, the cylinder didn't move.

"Jack, get in there," Kay directed. "No offense, AJ, but this is Jack's specialty," she joked.

"AJ, move aside." Jack flexed his bicep. "I got this."

AJ stepped back, giving him some room. Jack gripped the top edge with both hands, applied pressure, and forced the key right, then left. He felt it give. He strained and turned it one full rotation. "It's moving," Jack grunted.

As the key locked into position, creaking and popping noises echoed all around them. The walls trembled. Kay tried to pinpoint the source of the sounds. Then she saw it. On the outside edge of the mural, a seam between the frame and the picture was splitting open all the way around. And then—*pop*—a small gap appeared on the far right side. The noises died away. In the silence, the four friends stared at one another in astonishment.

Kay unfroze first. "It's a door! A sliding panel!" She scampered over to inspect it. The mural now rested in a groove cut into the ancient rock frame. Faint light shone through the gap from the other side. The door was only a half-inch thick. On the left side, an opening was cut into the wall so the whole panel could slide back.

"I knew this key would unlock something," AJ exulted. "Kay, does it slide over?"

She wedged her hand into the seam and tried to push the mural along the groove. It was stuck.

Jack ran over. "Here, let me help." He pushed hard, the door panel screeched, and then slowly slid into the surrounding stone. The pocket door was now halfway open, making a space wide enough for them to pass through.

"It's the secret chamber!" Eagle could barely contain his excitement. "Just like my grandfather said."

"Can you believe this?" Jack marveled.

"Let's go in," Kay pushed forward. "I see some light."

"Hold on, Kay," AJ hesitated. "Let's just take it slow."

"AJ, are you kidding me?" Kay countered. "We just discovered the secret chamber—the one that has been a legend for centuries. We're checking it out."

"I know," AJ replied. "But this place was kept secret for a reason. We need to be careful."

Kay paused. "Good point." She looked at everyone. "We'll take it slow."

The faint light beyond the door revealed a staircase that descended into the heart of the mesa. Kay led the way down. They breathed in warm, stale air as they went. After around ten feet, the stairs leveled off. At the far wall, light rays streamed through slits in a pile of rocks. Specks of dust floated in the air.

"So that's where the light's coming from!" Eagle exclaimed. "That opens to the outside. Hey, can you believe how big this place is?"

"Yeah, it's a big cave. Looks like it was mostly natural," AJ observed. "Whoever used it just dug out those steps from the mesa to get in."

"That doesn't look natural." Kay pointed to the far end of the chamber. "Someone definitely made that."

The friends walked over to investigate. Rocks piled along the back wall blocked what had once been a window. The frame, supported by two stone columns, had mostly collapsed. Sections of the columns lay broken on the floor.

"Whoa, looks like a cave-in," Jack said. Something glittery just above the debris-filled window frame of light caught his eye. "What's that?"

Kay climbed the rock pile to get a closer look. She shone her flashlight. "Holy cow!" Above the window, the remains of a three-dimensional clay mural were encased in a wooden boarder six feet wide by four feet tall. It hung directly above the window and was badly damaged. A glaze on the clay made it sparkle with a range of colors when the light hit it. Most of the middle and parts of the right side were either cracked or missing. She focused on the top left side, roughly a one-foot square piece that was still intact. Her face lit up.

"This is incredible!" Eagle beamed. "Only the elders were supposed to be able to get in here—and here we are." Eagle climbed the debris pile too and stood next to Kay. He studied the top left of the mural. "It's The Spires!" he exclaimed. He looked to her for confirmation. "Right?" The tall, slender columns of rock were clearly modeled. There were eight spires in all, each a different height. On the far left, a gold star marked the beginning of a silver trail that wound down the mountain, and then disappeared into the broken middle section.

"It's a map!" Kay beamed. "A 3D relief map." Kay pulled out her phone. She flipped through some images and then showed the screen to Eagle. "See! I've studied this area a million times. Those are definitely The Spires. It's the mountain range of Mount Fuego."

"A map?" Jack was skeptical. "It just looks like clay pieces with some glitter."

AJ chimed in. "Kay, I think you're right. The raised parts show mountain peaks and the lower ones show valleys." AJ too climbed the rock pile to get a closer look. "It even shows rivers and streams." He pointed to some blue lines. "It reminds me of those relief maps that hung on the wall in the third grade. You could feel the mountains and valleys on them. This is the same thing."

Kay took a photo and the three friends climbed down.

"But this is just a picture of The Spires that you've already researched a thousand times," Jack shrugged. "I don't see a trail."

"Maybe that's what the sparkly path is?" AJ offered. He directed everyone's attention to the silvery glaze that cut across the base of The Spires.

"Talon talked about the Tectonic legend and the powerful

rituals they performed at The Spires," Kay explained. "He also told us a secret chamber might hold key information to find a path up to them. This map has got to be it!"

Jack pointed to the blank middle section. "But if that's true, most of the pieces to the map are gone. If there was a secret way up, this map isn't telling us how to get there."

"It's here, Jack." Kay pointed to the rock pile. "All around us. Somehow the map cracked and fell out of its border. Even this top section that shows The Spire looks like it's about to fall." She looked at the fallen rock pile. "But the pieces must still here. We just need to find them."

"And put them together like a jigsaw puzzle," Eagle added.

"Exactly," Kay confirmed.

AJ kicked over some loose rocks in the debris pile. He knelt down. A sparkle caught his eye. "Here!" He called everyone over. "Here's one." He moved some small stones aside, revealing a clay fragment. It was about the size of playing card. One side was flat, but the other was raised and shiny. AJ moved another brick-sized rock, looking for more glittery pieces.

The friends joined AJ, searching for more clay pieces. They fanned out over the pile.

"Here's one!" Jack called. He showed it to Kay and Eagle.

AJ continued to turn over more rocks, working his way toward the debris-obstructed window. Once there, he cleared a space so he could poke his head through. More light shone in. "This must be the edge of the mesa—from inside."

"The cave-in must have blocked it all up a long time ago," Eagle said. "That's probably why this place was never discovered. You can't see it from the outside." He moved closer to AJ. "What's out there?"

AJ peered down. He got a little dizzy. "A two-hundred-foot drop—all the way to the river." He shuddered and pulled his head back in. "Scary."

"Let me see." Kay worked her way over and pushed herself into position. She gingerly put her head through. "Wow! That's some view." She looked down toward a river below. Scattered down the steep slope, a few sparkles caught her eye. "More pieces are down there!" she exclaimed. "They must have fallen out when the window frame broke. You can see a glittery trail all the way to the river." She pulled her head back inside.

Meanwhile, Jack had been inspecting the cave-in between the interior columns. He studied the fragment AJ had found in the debris pile. "I wish this thing wasn't broken," Jack grumbled. "It does look like a jigsaw piece." He turned it in the light. "If they were together, I guess we would know for sure if it was really a map to The Spires."

Kay walked over. She reached for the fragment in Jack's hand. "It's a map, Jack." She was confident. "And it's all here—in these pieces. We just need to collect them all and put them back together."

"Well, I'm pretty good at puzzles," Jack bragged. "Like carnival games."

"It's good to have a talent!" Kay joked.

"But there's a ton of jumbled pieces here," AJ said. "And lots have fallen out the window. We'd need to collect those, too."

"We'll get it done, AJ," Kay assured him. "It wouldn't be

fun if it was easy, right?" She smiled. "A secret passage to The Spires," she beamed. "Let's come back tomorrow with all the climbing gear. We'll be able to collect the pieces that fell down the slope. We can do it."

"Okay," AJ said. "But let's keep what we found up here a secret—for now. Who knows what this place really is? We don't want other people poking around."

"I agree," Jack said. "Don't tell anyone. Let's come back tomorrow. We'll need all day to find like maybe a hundred jigsaw pieces and put them back together."

⊛ CHAPTER 13 ⊛

The next day they arrived early at the mesa. There was no one else there, just as they had hoped. Kay had brought her climbing equipment. She planned to lower herself out the chamber window and make her way down the slope, collecting the clay fragments as she went. Jack would hold the rope to secure her, while Eagle would keep watch and direct her. Meanwhile, AJ would search for any fragments left inside. He was sure he would get dizzy if he had to lean out the window to guide Kay.

As Kay and Jack set up the ropes and anchors, AJ and Eagle cleared away the fallen rocks that blocked the window.

"Hey, Jack, that's big enough for even you to get through," Eagle teased.

Jack ignored him.

Eagle stuck his head out. "Yep, I can see the pieces. Good thing they catch the light." He inspected the boulder field that covered the slope. "Kay, be careful. Some of those rocks don't look too stable, especially near the cliff. It's a straight drop to the river."

"I'll be okay." She brushed off Eagle's concerns as she secured her harness. "Jack's got me on the rope." She gave Jack a stern look. "Right?"

"What was that?" Jack chuckled.

"Yeah, yeah." She tied the rope to her belt. "I'll try to collect as many pieces as I can. Seriously, Jack. Are you ready?"

Jack made sure that the rope was securely threaded through the belay device on his belt.

Eagle squinted at it. "How does that thing work again?"

"Friction," Jack explained. "The rope snaps tight through this figure-eight loop here. It can hold a lot of weight—even a couple of me." He smiled. "Kay, you ready?"

"On belay," she called.

"The belay is on," Jack confirmed. This exchange was a tradition among climbers. "You're free to climb—climb away."

With that, Kay pushed backward through the window onto the rockslide. Jack had anchored himself to a boulder inside and watched Kay carefully as she descended.

Eagle too was watching. He mapped out a route for her to follow. "To the left," he called. "There's one right there."

Fully secured to Jack, Kay moved confidently, closing in on the glazed piece. But her feet slipped on the loose stones, sending a few rocks skittering down the steep slope and over the cliff. She steadied herself and reached for the fragment. "Got it!" She blew the dust off it and put it in her backpack. "Where's the next one?"

"That way," Eagle directed. "About three feet down.

Lower her a bit, Jack."

Jack let out some slack.

"Is that one?" Kay asked, pointing.

"Yeah, yeah. That's one," Eagle confirmed. "By that big square boulder."

Kay made her way over.

Meanwhile, back inside, AJ was digging through the rubble from the cave-in. He found more fragments. One side of each was shiny and textured. Given the full size of the mural, he estimated that they would need to collect about seventy pieces in all. He was curious about what they would reveal when they were assembled.

AJ went over to the window to check on Kay's progress. "How's it going?"

"Good," Eagle said. "She's found a bunch. Luckily most of them are small enough to fit in her pack. How about you?"

"I found a few. I think most of them fell outside during the cave-in. But I was able to remove these ones still attached to the wooden boarder. I wanted to make sure they didn't fall down and break. I set them over there." He motioned to the middle of the room.

"I hope we can put them all together," Jack chimed in while still concentrating on Kay.

"We will," AJ said. "It may take some time, but we'll get it done."

"Hey, what's that sound?" Eagle cocked his head, straining to listen. "It sounds like..." Eagle paused. "Oh no. Voices! Someone's coming!" He darted from side to side, not knowing what to do.

"We're going to be discovered—all this stuff—and Kay's

hanging off the cliff!" AJ talked fast. "We're going to get into so much trouble."

"Slow down, slow down," Jack snapped. "Take it easy. We're not discovered yet." Jack was forceful. "You two go out there and distract them, whoever they are. Keep them away from the chamber door and definitely on the far side of the mesa. We don't want them to see Kay swinging down the slope."

"But Jack, you're the sweet-talker!" Eagle protested.

"I'm all 'tied up' here. You have to do it. Go!"

Eagle and AJ raced across the chamber and bounded up the steps to the pocket door at the top. They had left it open just a bit. But if visitors started poking around, they might notice it.

Eagle and AJ slid the door open so they could exit. Eagle ran out and quietly ascended the stairs. He peered around the stone wall and spied two girls arriving. "Good, just some hikers." He raced back down to the keyhole in the floor, where AJ was hovering over the submerged key.

"Get the key out before they see it," Eagle called.

With his heart racing, AJ grabbed the key and twisted it, but it wouldn't budge. "Eagle," he hissed. "Help me!"

Eagle knelt next to AJ. He took a deep breath. They both yanked feverishly at the metal key stuck in the hole.

"They're coming this way," Eagle worried. "AJ, you have to get this thing out and go back in and close that door behind you. Use that sunblock trick again. Do it. I'll head them off."

Eagle raced toward the hikers. They were checking out one of the smaller stone dwelling only a few yards away. He paused behind a wall, closed his eyes, and tried to calm himself. Then he turned the corner and spoke to them. "Welcome to the mesa! I'm a volunteer Junior Park Ranger. I'm happy to answer any questions you might have."

The hikers, caught off guard by his sudden appearance, flinched.

"Did you notice those stones over there?" Eagle pointed to the far side of the mesa and steered the hikers away from AJ.

AJ could hear Eagle acting like a real tour guide: "And over here you can see... And over there is the...." It reminded him of how Jack talked to guests at his father's restaurants. "Those two are spending way too much time together," he thought.

Meanwhile, AJ had refocused his efforts on trying to dislodge the key. Although he was trying to stay calm, he broke into a sweat. He could hear Eagle's tour getting nearer. He needed to move now, or he would be discovered. He pushed, pulled, jiggled, and twisted—and the key suddenly popped out! He fell backward, landing on his bottom. Surprised but relieved, he got up and raced back toward the door and squeezed through the opening. Once in, he slid the door completely shut. There was a muffled thud as it sealed. AJ exhaled. "That was close." He ran back down the steps, careful not to fall in the dusky light, to find Jack.

"I think we're okay," AJ called out as he entered. "Jack, I shut the door." He was breathing heavily. "Eagle's up there. He sounds like you." AJ chuckled. "Hopefully he'll keep them away from the edge of the mesa."

"I'm sure he will," Jack agreed. "He's a real charmer." Then he paused. "AJ. You said you shut the chamber door?"

"Yes. Yes, I did. No one saw me or the secret passage."

"All the way?"

"Yes. We're okay. We just have to lie low till those hikers leave." AJ was proud of his efforts.

"That's good, AJ. Really good." Jack paused. "Except for one thing. You're still holding the key. You just locked us in."

AJ looked at the key in his hand and slumped. "*Uhh!*" he groaned.

"It'll be okay," Jack laughed. "We'll figure something out. Even if we have to go out this way." He pointed to the window.

"Great," AJ muttered.

Meanwhile, Kay was wrapping up. AJ and Jack kept hoping that Eagle would keep anyone from seeing her from above. She collected a few last pieces and placed them in her pack. It was now heavy, being full of jagged clay pieces. It weighed her down. Tightening the straps around her shoulders, she scanned the rockslide to plan her ascent. She moved quickly and gracefully up toward the window. She was careful not make too much noise or disturb too many loose stones. Within moments she had arrived and climbed in.

"This thing's heavy." She set her backpack on the ground next to Jack. "AJ, did you find many pieces in here?"

"A few," he replied. "Now we just need to put them together."

"Where's Eagle?" Kay started to loosen her rope knot.

"Hold on." Jack stopped her. "AJ locked us in here. You'll need to climb up with the key and reopen the door."

Kay glared at AJ. "You locked us in here? How did that happen?"

"It's a long story." AJ spoke sheepishly. "But Eagle's up

there distracting a bunch of hikers."

There was an awkward silence.

"Okay then." Kay retied her knot. "Let me make sure I have the right gear and then I'll head up. Hopefully I won't be discovered when I pop over the edge. Right, AJ?" she joked.

"Maybe we should just wait until the hikers leave," AJ said. "We don't want to be discovered."

"No one's going to see me, AJ. And for all we know, they might already have left. That door's so thick, Eagle could be knocking on it and we'd never hear him. I'm going up."

"Fine." AJ handed her his backpack. The metal key was inside. "You'll need this."

"Got it. Jack, you ready? On belay?" Kay craned her neck out the window and looked up. Above her was a sheer cliff, unlike the slanting boulder field below. At the top was a large overhang. She studied the terrain, mapping out the best route.

"The belay is on, Kay. Climb away," Jack instructed.

Kay stepped outside, this time heading up toward the top of the mesa. Since she was ascending, she needed to place her protection equipment into cracks on the rock face. After she secured each anchor, she attached a spring-action metal-clip carabiner and looped the rope through. She secured several such carabiners as she climbed.

On a small ledge below the steepest part of the overhang, Kay paused and reached for some chalk powder to dry her hands. The chalk bag was clipped to the back of her harness. She reached for a tiny bump on the rock face and held on tight. Once her hands were secure, she inched her feet up, compacting her body in preparation for a controlled lunge.

She had spied a solid hand-hold directly below the edge of the mesa. "That's a bomber hold," she muttered. "It's huge." She took a deep breath and flung herself toward it. Flying like a squirrel leaping from a tree, she grabbed the hold squarely. She swung her legs to the rock and pushed herself up to a secure perch. She was now right under the top of the mesa.

"How does she do that?" AJ asked in awe. "She just flew through the air!"

"I know. Crazy," Jack smiled.

From her position, Kay could now see Eagle. He had spotted her too but didn't let on. He kept up a stream of chatter to distract the hikers, who stared at him, open mouthed, as he pointed out details of the ruins. "And over here was a special ritual site…. And over there…." She wasn't sure if anything he was saying was true. He ushered the hikers toward one of the ruins on the other side of the mesa, far from Kay. "…And look at that view!"

Seizing the opportunity, she flung her feet up and onto the top. Kneeling out of sight, she quickly untied the rope. She gave it a big yank and then threw it over the side for Jack to reel in. She wiped her hands to remove the chalk and then slipped out of her harness. She placed it in her backpack. She re-tied her long hair in a ponytail and walked over to join Eagle. He smiled as he saw her appear.

"Well, we certainly are busy today," Eagle said. "Your first time at the mesa?"

Kay smiled. "Yeah, I was just 'hanging out'—decided to come over."

"Great! We're moving to that building over there." Eagle winked to show he caught her pun.

Kay joined in.

After a thorough tour, Eagle waved goodbye to his new friends, and he and Kay wandered off to the side. "I don't know if they're leaving any time soon," Eagle said. "They're really into this stuff."

"You were playing the tour guide pretty well," Kay laughed.

Eagle blushed. "Yeah, I really got into it. Then it dawned upon me that AJ had the key and I told him to shut the door behind him. I was wondering how long I would have to keep it up. I figured you'd have to climb up to unlock the door. Was it a hard climb?"

"A little bit. The last section was tough."

"For you? Wow. That says a lot."

Now she blushed. "Hey, this place is popular today. Here comes another group," Kay said. "You'll have to charm these guys, too."

"I guess you're right. Let's head them off before they get too close to the door. We'll need to keep AJ and Jack down there till everyone's gone. It may be all day," he joked.

"Oh, no." There was a mischievous glint in her eye. "We wouldn't want to do that."

⊛ CHAPTER 14 ⊛

"**A**re you going to have some ribs with your sauce?" Kay joked. Jack had squirted sauce all over the side of his plate. "Why don't you just drink the bottle?" They were at AJ's house in his workroom. They had swung by Fiery Bill's to get some take-out to satisfy Jack.

Jack focused on his meal. "Hey, you guys left us down there for a couple hours. I'm hungry."

"There were like eight groups that came by," Kay giggled.

"Yeah, right." AJ shook his head. "Well, at least we weren't discovered."

"Yeah, that's what's important." Eagle winked at Kay and laughed.

"I guess." Jack squeezed some more sauce onto his plate.

"Well, it looks like we have a real mystery on our hands." Eagle chomped a rib. "We have a Native tribe that made a key that opened an underground chamber with a totally broken clay mural that could be a map that could hold some clues about an ancient legend. Right?"

"Good recap," AJ smiled. "Well, it's time now to put the jigsaw pieces together to see what we've got."

AJ had collected all the fragments they had found and arranged them, shiny side up, on the floor. They had also carefully removed the remaining parts of the relief map that was still hanging above the window in the chamber. Many of these pieces were close to falling down, and they couldn't risk them breaking or falling out the open window.

"How do we begin to assemble this thing?" Jack asked.

"I thought you were good at this stuff, Jack. Start with the ones that have the same color and go from there," Kay instructed.

"Also, look for pieces that have the same ridges and grooves on them," AJ added. "Remember, it's a relief map. We need to line up the mountains and valleys. We can use the current maps of the area as a guide." He pulled up a relief map of the Mount Fuego range on his laptop.

The four friends studied the fragments. The edges were jagged: the fragments looked like pieces of a smashed plate. Only a few had silver markings on them.

"Here's a match!" Jack connected two pieces. Together they modeled a mountain ridge.

"And here's another one." Eagle reached over and fit a couple more pieces together. He studied the image on AJ's laptop to see if he could figure out what part of the landscape they represented.

The friends worked for most of the afternoon. As they connected more and more pieces, the map and trail became clearer. The silver trail followed a river through a valley, from the base of the mountain range up toward a ridge. But after that, a large chunk of the map was still missing. In the next section for which they had pieces, the silver trail picked up again, following a cliff just below The Spires.

After adding more pieces around the map's edges, the friends could identify each of the eight rock columns that made up The Spires. Their tips on the map were at different heights, just like in real life.

Kay polished the shiny gold star just to the left of the last rock spire. "The trail definitely ends here." She looked at her friends. "Can there really be something there?" she wondered.

Eagle knelt down next to her. He studied the image, too. "I hope so," Eagle said. Kay and Eagle smiled in amazement. They turned and looked for more matches, eager to see what would be revealed next.

The right side of the map, too, started to fill in. A high ridge ringed a large, deep basin. Several streams collected water from higher elevations and flowed into a river that cut through the valley just over the basin's edge.

AJ traced the river system. "That must be the beginning of the El Gato River. All of the town's water comes from there." He surveyed the remaining fragments on the floor and grew concerned. "I think we're still missing a lot. Especially here in the middle."

"Are you sure?" Jack had just found another match.

"Yes," AJ nodded. "There's just not enough. And most of the pieces don't have the silver trail."

"Let's put together as much as we can, AJ," Eagle said

encouragingly. "The trail is definitely clear around The Spires and in this river valley below. Maybe we don't need all of them. Just enough to point us in the right direction."

"Maybe." AJ was skeptical. He grabbed another fragment. "Okay, let's go as far as we can."

The friends continued to assemble what they could. By late afternoon it was clear they didn't have enough pieces.

"I can't believe after all this work, this map still shows nothing useful," Jack bemoaned. "This whole middle section contains the information we need."

AJ shook his head in disappointment. "I agree, Jack. I think we're stuck. But we do have a lot of information here." He reached for his modern map. "We know what this landscape looks like. Maybe we can start the trail with what we have and see where it goes?"

"I don't think that's going to work," Kay said. "I've studied this area a thousand times. The terrain is rugged—lots of cliffs. Without the actual trail to guide us, we'd just be wandering aimlessly."

"Maybe my grandfather can help us?" Eagle offered. "He knows the legend better than anyone. He may know where to look. Maybe there's something we missed up at the mesa?"

"That's a great idea," AJ said. "Plus we need to tell him we found the secret chamber. I can't believe we haven't called him sooner. He's gonna be so excited."

"Give him a call, Eagle," Kay directed. "See if he's around."

Eagle walked over to a quiet corner and called his grandfather.

Moments later he rejoined them. "Talon's headed to the town center for that big meeting with the mayor—to discuss the earthquakes and evacuation."

"Oh yeah," AJ nodded. "I forgot all about that."

"He said we should meet him and show him what we found," Eagle said. "He was all fired up to see it." He continued, "Kay, take a picture of what we have so far. AJ, grab a few jigsaw pieces. I told him we'd meet at the wind sculpture."

AJ put a few fragments in his backpack. "Okay. We need a break anyway. Let's go and hear what the mayor has to say."

From AJ's house, the friends rode their bikes into town. Everybody was filing into the square. Eagle spotted Kay and Jack's parents on the far side, near the podium where the mayor was to speak. AJ's mom was with them. "There's Talon." He pointed him out. "Right under the sculpture." The friends pushed through the crowd. It thinned out at the sculpture.

Talon was smiling as they approached. The sculpture twisted above their heads. The spiral design made it appear that the reflective pieces flowed up and down as it spun. They all huddled together. "So you found the secret chamber?" Talon kept his voice low. "You all are amazing. I've been up at that mesa many times over the years and I've never found anything. Please show me pictures." He could barely contain his excitement.

Kay handed him her phone. Talon studied the pictures of the underground chamber and the broken relief map. "Just like the stories my father told me," he beamed. "Are those The Spires?" He zoomed in. "Unbelievable."

"Yes." Eagle answered for all of them. "We think it's a map to get up there! But the trail section isn't complete yet. We've collected as many broken pieces as we could find, and we're putting them back together at AJ's house. Kay, show him what we have so far."

Kay showed Talon the photo.

"Did you tell anyone else about this?" Talon asked.

"No," Eagle answered. "We closed the chamber up tight, and no one but us knows about the map."

"Good," Talon nodded.

"The problem is, we're still missing pieces," AJ said. He reached into his bag and pulled out some clay fragments. "This is what they look like. Have you ever seen anything like these before?"

AJ handed a few over. Talon inspected both sides.

"We were wondering if maybe there was another secret chamber up at the mesa?" AJ added. "Or did the Tectonic legend mention anything else about the map?"

The wrinkles around Talon's eyes grew deep as he flashed a bright smile. He looked up for a few seconds and then toward the kids. "You guys can save the whole area—just like the Tectonic did five hundred years ago." He drew them closer. "All these people"—he spread his arms wide. "You are so close to the answers," he beamed. "Stay right here and listen carefully when the mayor speaks."

"Shouldn't we get a little closer?" Kay asked. "He's speaking at the other end of the square."

"No," Talon insisted. "Stay here. It's important—and listen."

With that, Talon handed the tiles back to AJ and turned to leave.

"You're not going to stay for the mayor?" Eagle asked.

"Listen carefully, Eagle." Talon repeated. He was still smiling as he disappeared into the crowd.

"Talk about a dramatic exit," Jack said. "And he didn't even answer AJ's question about the Tectonic legend and map. Why does he have to be so mysterious?"

"That's how he is." Eagle defended him. "But this is a little odder than usual."

"Listen carefully to the mayor's speech?" Jack shook his head. "Don't we need to find more tiles? How is the mayor's speech going to help us with that?" He looked at AJ.

The mayor stepped up onto the stage to address the crowd.

"I don't know, Jack," AJ replied. "I really don't."

⊛ CHAPTER 15 ⊛

The mayor began to speak. The crowd listened intently. "I can barely hear him from back here," Jack complained. "This sculpture is making too much noise. I'm going to move up."

"Talon said to stay here to listen," Kay reminded him.

"Yeah, but we can't hear anything from back here. Who knows what he's saying?" Jack bolted to get closer to the podium.

"Jack's right." AJ strained to listen to the mayor. "This whirling is making it difficult to hear." But AJ didn't follow Jack. Instead, AJ stared up at the wind sculpture. It whooshed as it spun.

"But Talon said stay here," Kay repeated. She watched Jack leave.

AJ continued to stare in silence at the spinning sculpture.

"What's up, AJ? I've seen that look before." She and

Eagle looked up, too. At first they didn't understand. They watched the pieces twirling and sparkling.

AJ reached for one of the fragments he had brought with him. He silently shared it with Kay and Eagle. They smiled.

Moments later Jack returned. "What's up?" Jack called. "I have no clue what the mayor's saying. Underground pressure? Seismic something?" He was frustrated. "What are you guys looking at?"

The three friends continued to stare up in silence.

"Am I missing something?" Jack asked. "What's going on?"

"It's hidden in plain sight," Kay whispered. She could barely contain herself.

"What's hidden in plain sight?" Jack scratched his head. "What are you guys taking about?"

"The jigsaw pieces," AJ whispered. He pointed up. "From the sculpture. Those are the missing pieces! The fragments must have fallen out of the chamber all the way down to the river. Remember, that's where the plaque said the artist found them. Talon must have realized that when I handed the pieces to him."

Jack looked up, confused. "Those are the missing pieces to the jigsaw puzzle? I mean the map? Are you serious? They've been here the whole time—for like fifty years?"

"Yes," Kay answered. "They're right here."

"But they're not just going to let us just take them," Eagle frowned. "It's a major work—here for everyone."

"Maybe we don't have to," AJ said. He studied the spinning sculpture. "I have an idea."

⊛ CHAPTER 16 ⊛

"**S**o AJ. What's the plan?" Kay asked.

They were back at AJ's house. He was moving books and boxes, clearing a path to his 3D printer. "We're going to use this," he said with confidence, moving it into position.

"This?" Jack looked bewildered. "What is it?"

"It prints 3D objects," AJ said.

"Any object?" Jack asked.

"Yeah, pretty much." AJ reached for a plastic phone docking station on his desk. "I made this the other day. All you need is a picture of something, then you put it through special software." He held up his laptop. "The software gives it depth. And we need that here because of the peaks and valleys on those pieces."

"So you take a picture of something and then print it?" Jack studied the printer.

"Yes," AJ said. "It's pretty cool. You can make all kinds of stuff. You just need to put it through the software."

"I'm sure the printer will print what we need, AJ, but how are we going to get pictures of the clay fragments on the wind sculpture?" Eagle asked. "The sculpture's ten feet tall in the middle of a busy square. What are we going to say? We're cleaning it?"

"I've got an idea—it's really simple." Jack spoke up. "If anyone asks, we'll say we're doing a school project about public art or something. We won't harm the sculpture. We're just going to take close-up pictures."

"Wouldn't we need a ladder?" Eagle countered. "That thing's pretty tall."

"Yes, but hey I've got an idea! We can get one from a vendor at the farmers' market," Jack said. "They bring them to set up their tents and stuff. Don't worry. I'll get one."

"If you say so, Jack." Eagle was still skeptical.

"Let's meet there tomorrow right as the market is ending. That's the best time." Jack looked at AJ. "Do we need a special camera?"

"Yes, I'll use my mom's. We need something with more resolution than a phone camera."

"Great!" Jack said. "Let's get it done."

The next day the friends all met up at the wind sculpture. As expected, vendors were closing out their sales and taking down their tents.

"Jack, do you see anyone with a ladder?" Kay asked.

Jack surveyed the square.

"There. At the burrito stand." Jack pointed. "That's good luck, too. I'll buy one while I'm over there." He strolled over, eager to eat his meal.

Kay turned to Eagle. "He is such a sweet-talker. Just like you up at the mesa." She laughed.

Eagle blushed. "No one's as good as him."

Moments later Jack returned. He had a stepladder balanced on his shoulder while he scarfed down his burrito. His words were muffled. "See. This is perfect." Bits of rice fell from his mouth.

"You're so gross, Jack." Kay shook her head in disgust. "Set it up over here," she directed. "And AJ, hand me the camera."

AJ did so.

Jack set the stepladder right under the sculpture. The clay pieces twisted and sparkled above. Kay started climbing the rungs. Within seconds, Sheriff Cole walked over.

Everyone knew the sheriff. And he knew everyone, too. He was in full uniform but also carrying groceries that he had just bought at the market. He cleared his throat. "Can I ask what you guys are doing?" Sheriff Cole stared directly at Kay, who was halfway up the ladder. His low, authoritative voice stopped Kay in her tracks.

Jack stepped forward. "Hey Sheriff." He stuck with his plan. "We're doing a project. Well, Eagle is," he clarified. "He's making a wind sculpture similar to this one—for school. He wants to impress his art teacher for next year. Right, Eagle?"

Eagle nodded, tongue-tied.

"He doesn't seem like the arty type, but he is." Jack laughed. "We're helping him get some ideas with these pictures."

"Great!" Sheriff Cole replied. "I love this thing, too." He looked up at the sculpture. "The way it sparkles. It's very striking. Eagle, do you do a lot of art?"

There was a long pause. Jack stared at Eagle, willing him to answer. He finally did. "Oh yeah. Mostly Native American stuff—with my grandfather."

"Sounds good," Sheriff Cole said. "I'd like to see your work some time. Again, I love this piece. I pass it everyday. It always amazes me, how fast it spins. You know, you can see it from miles away."

They all nodded, remembering that they had seen it spinning from Devil's Drop.

"Hey, what teacher are you doing the project for?" Sheriff Cole asked.

Eagle thought quickly. He said the first teacher's name that popped into his head. "Ms. —he stammered—"uh, Ms. Lody."

"Really?" Sheriff Cole's eyes grew wide. "That's amazing! Y'know, she's my niece. I can't wait to tell her that I saw one of her students doing a project for her. She'll be so happy."

"Wait, wait." Eagle fumbled. He started to sweat. "You can't tell her."

"What?" Sheriff Cole asked, confused.

Jack stepped forward. "What he means is that he's doing it as an extra credit project and he wants it to be a surprise. He's going to bring it in during the first week of school. If you can just hold off talking about it with her till then, he'd really appreciate it."

There was an awkward silence; then Sheriff Cole spoke. "Okay, no problem," he nodded. "I'm not seeing her for the rest of the summer. Maybe, after school starts, I'll ask her if I can see it." He chuckled.

"Hey Sheriff." Jack smiled. He turned on his charm. "Do you think it'll be okay if we stopped the sculpture from spinning just for a few seconds. Y'know, so we can get some clear pictures? As an art lover, I'm sure you can certainly understand we'd want to be true to the original piece."

"Absolutely," Sheriff Cole nodded. "Just start it back up when you're done. Again, I can't wait to see what you create." With that, Sheriff Cole turned and headed out of the square. He called out as he walked. "Hey, take care, guys, and stay safe on that ladder."

"Will do," Kay replied.

They all let out a sigh of relief.

"Great." Eagle slumped. "Now I have to do a real project for Ms. Lody before school even starts. And the Sheriff's gonna want to see it. Who knew he was an art fan? Unbelievable." Eagle shook his head.

"Hey, I'm sorry, but I had to come up with something," Jack said. "You just stood there. I didn't want us to get caught. At least I bought you some time. Right?"

"Yeah, yeah, I guess. But what are the odds his niece is Ms. Lody?" Eagle continued to shake his head. "I should've picked a different name."

"It'll be okay, Eagle." AJ put his arm around him. "Don't worry. I'll help you get it done." He turned to Kay. "What's important is that we get these photos and print them out. Kay, take them quickly and let's get back to work."

⊛ CHAPTER 17 ⊛

"This thing's really amazing." Jack was mesmerized by the 3D printer. Following a specific pattern, a thin stream of hot plastic oozed from the stylus. It moved back and forth in layers over the printer platform. After a short while, a replica of a clay piece from the sculpture had been formed.

"We're ready for another one," Jack called. He carefully removed the newly printed piece with needle-nose pliers and placed it on a rack to cool. "One down, nineteen to go!"

"At least we have them all now, right?" AJ said. "Kay, mark the spot where the silver trail is in the photo. This way we'll see the path all the way to The Spires."

Kay ripped off a small square of aluminum foil and gripped it firmly with tweezers. She studied the photo of the original clay fragment on the wind sculpture. She looked for the exact spot on which to place the foil on the newly printed plastic tile. She lined it up and glued it in place. She waited a few moments for the glue to set and then moved the tile aside to work on another one.

Meanwhile, AJ loaded another image into his computer. He sent the signal to the printer. The stylus started to move, layering another puzzle piece.

After several hours of working in this way, they had managed to recreate all the wind sculpture pieces from their photos. The friends hovered over them, searching for matches. As more and more of them came together, the missing section of the relief map filled in. Eagle grabbed the final piece. He completed the puzzle.

There was a moment of silence. Then they all celebrated.

"The trail to The Spires!" AJ exclaimed.

Eagle and Jack exchanged high-fives.

Kay traced the silver route with her hand. In the new section the trail veered away from the main river following a small tributary up a steep incline and then disappeared. She frowned. "Where'd it go? It just ends."

"Yes, but it picks up again here"—Eagle pointed—"higher up on this ridge. But you're right: There's a gap."

Kay studied the fully assembled map. She paused. "I know that area." She reached for AJ's laptop and zoomed in on where the trail disappeared. She tilted her head, confused. "I remember this," she mused. "There's a waterfall there—a tall one." She noted the elevation markings. "It's spectacular, but I've never seen a way up to its top."

"We would need to climb up a waterfall?" AJ asked.

"Maybe," Kay replied. "It's hard to say. I know how to get to its base, but climbing it, we'll just have to see."

"Well the trail clearly picks up at the top of the falls," Eagle noted. "And after that, higher up, it crosses this river and heads up this peak here."

"We're going to need all our climbing gear, Jack," Kay said. "Some of these cliffs look pretty steep."

Jack nodded. "We might also need wet suits."

"Wait a minute," Eagle got everyone's attention. "There looks like a huge drop off right here. Up the mountain from the river crossing."

"Great," AJ muttered. "I was hoping for a simple path."

"Like I've said, AJ"—Kay put her arm on his shoulder—"no one's been able to get to these spires. At least no one in the past few hundred years. If this really is a path up to them, it won't be easy."

"What's all this stuff here?" Jack pointed to the right side of the map.

Off the main river, at the higher elevation, deep in the basin that they had noted earlier, was a smudge on the clay tile. The picture covered a large area on the far rock wall ringing the basin. Jack moved in closer to get a better look, but the colors had faded. "I wonder what that is," he said.

AJ grabbed the laptop and zoomed in. "It's a pretty big basin, that's for sure. But this doesn't show anything more than that."

"The only way to find out is to go," Kay said. "I can't wait! We have a chance to get up to The Spires and unlock the mystery of the Tectonic legend—The 'Song of the Mountain.' Are you guys ready?"

"Oh yeah!" They were.

Eagle added, "I wouldn't miss it for the world."

⚜ CHAPTER 18 ⚜

The next day, the four friends headed to the Mount Fuego range. They rode bikes on the dirt road next to the El Gato River. Kay had previously been to the waterfall shown on their ancient map. Getting to its base would be straightforward, but how they would get up it was still a mystery.

They had taken a picture of their ancient map and printed it out to bring with them. They also brought a copy of a more modern map of the area.

The landscape was rugged: rock outcroppings surrounded them. From towering peaks on either side, streams flowed down into the river.

"We have to get back before dark," Eagle reminded them. "It wouldn't be safe to be out here then, plus my grandfather's making his fiery chili for you, Jack."

Jack's eyes lit up. "Man, I love that stuff."

"So let's stick to the trail," Eagle continued, "and keep

focused on getting up to The Spires."

They all agreed.

"Isn't this place beautiful?" Kay said admiringly. "And check out those cliffs in front of us. They have to be over a hundred feet tall."

"Do we have to climb those?" AJ asked.

"At some point we do," Kay replied bluntly. "The trail definitely makes its way to the top of the waterfall. It's not too far from here, and hopefully we'll figure out a way up when we get there."

The friends continued their trek. The path became steeper as it approached the cliffs. They had hiked for about two hours and had penetrated deep into the mountain range. After they climbed a steep hill, they all stopped.

"Do you hear that?" Eagle asked.

"Sounds like water," Jack said. "Lots of it. Right over this ridge." He ran up. Once he had reached the top, droplets of water pelted him as he looked out.

Kay, Eagle, and AJ ran up, too. The four friends surveyed the view. In front of them was a towering waterfall. AJ estimated that it was over a hundred feet high. In the mist surrounding it, a rainbow shimmered.

"See what I mean?" Kay was awestruck. "Amazing right?"

"This view is worth the hike," Eagle said. "It's incredible that this ancient map is so accurate. It's really here."

"That's true," AJ observed, "but this is also where the trail ends."

"There's got to be something around here," Kay said. "The old map has been accurate up till now. The trail can't just stop here. We know it picks up somewhere on top of this cliff." She looked up at the sheer rock wall. "Let's get closer."

They climbed the rocks along the bank of the river until they reached the base of the cliff. A powerful, ten-foot wide stream of water flowed off its top to the river below. They were only a few yards from the pounding water.

From the side of the falls Jack looked up. "You're right Kay, this place is unbelievable!" He spread his arms feeling the spray of water as it damped his clothes.

AJ studied the landscape. "There's no way I'm getting up this thing," he said flatly.

"Me too," Eagle added. "That's a major cliff. Not to mention the waterfall."

Kay inched closer to the falls. "There's got to be a path up this thing."

"Why?" Jack asked. "Maybe the Tectonic were super climbers."

"Because scaling a cliff this tall and steep is too much even for me," Kay admitted. "They were tribal elders—not superhuman."

Eagle stood next to Kay. "So you think there might be a path up?"

"It's worth a look," she replied. She pointed through the pounding water to a spot behind the falls. "There's a gap back there—a small cave. See it? Looks like the force of the pounding water created it. Let's check it out."

AJ walked up next to Kay and Eagle. "Hey, I do see it. It looks pretty cool," he said. "My mom has been to these fancy hotels that have cafes built behind man-made waterfalls. She showed me pictures. They looked kinda like that."

Jack joined them. "Well, let's get behind the water and

check it out."

The friends entered the river and waded up to the side of the falls. They made their way to an underwater ledge. As they got closer to the crashing water, they could see that the pool under the waterfall was very deep. The strength of the water had carved out a portion of the bedrock and base of the cliff. They followed the ledge around until it brought them behind the falls. The water pounded and splashed, soaking them thoroughly.

"It's so loud!" Eagle yelled over the roar. His wet clothes stuck to his body as he inched along the back wall and into cave. Kay was already inside wringing out her long braid. She was standing in the water at the back end of the cave where the water was waist deep.

"This place is amazing!" she called to Eagle as he entered. Beads of water covered her face.

Within a few moments, AJ and Jack joined them.

"Holy cow!" Jack surveyed the cave. "You're right, AJ. This place is big enough to set up a few tables. I should tell my dad about this for a restaurant idea." He sloshed through the water to the back wall. He noticed a ledge just above the water line that ringed the entire cave. It was around a foot wide. He removed his pack and balanced it up on the ledge. The other followed.

"I love the way my voice sounds in here." AJ shouted to hear his voice bounce off the walls. "Echo!" He surveyed the cave. "But I don't see a trail up that gets us up the cliff." He put his hand on the ledge and pulled himself out of the water. His feet dangled just at the water line as he sat. He peered out through the falls in front of him. The pounding water echoed in the cave, mixing with his friends' voices.

"There's got to be something here," Kay said hopefully. "I just know it." She too pulled herself onto the ledge and carefully walked toward the far side of the waterfall from the inside of the cave. For balance, she grabbed the roots of sporadic plants that covered the back wall. Light shone through the wall of water, casting eerie shadows everywhere.

Eagle stayed in the water, sticking close to the back wall. He hoped to find some marker or clue.

Jack too stayed in the water. He waded closer to the falls. He was curious to see how deep the pool was and if there was an underwater cavern or a secret entrance underneath the pounding water. He moved closer to investigate.

"Be careful, Jack," AJ called from his perch on the ledge. The roar of the falls made it difficult to hear. "Don't get hit with that water. It'll hurt."

Jack continued walking toward the waterfall.

"Jack!" AJ screamed. "It gets really deep right there, too. Stop!"

The echoing noises made it impossible for AJ to get Jack's attention.

AJ pushed hard off the back wall, hoping to get enough momentum to intercept Jack. As he pushed off, he grabbed some loose plants from the back wall. The roots formed a muddy ball. Seeing Jack in danger, right at the point where the pool became very deep, he threw the wadded mud at him. It landed square on his back. Jack stopped in his tracks and turned around.

AJ screamed to him as he made eye contact. "Stop! The water's really deep right there!"

Jack just stared at AJ. AJ grew concerned that Jack was hurt—or mad.

Eagle, witnessing the exchange, made his way over to Jack. "Are you okay? AJ was trying to warn you about the deep water."

"Hey, I was just trying to help you," AJ insisted. "Don't be mad. You could have gotten hurt."

Jack looked intently in AJ's direction. He waded back through the water toward him.

"Jack, I'm sorry. Really," AJ pleaded. "I didn't want you to get hurt."

Jack moved up next to AJ then reached behind him to the back wall. He had spied something unusual: a small hole the size of a fist where AJ had grabbed the mud. It was right above the ledge, a few feet up above the waterline.

"I'm not mad, AJ. I think I found something!" Jack exclaimed. He sloshed over to his pack and reached for a collapsible hiking pole. He moved back over to AJ. "Look." He extended the pole and stuck it into the small opening.

Eagle and Kay made their way over. "What is it?" Kay asked.

Jack rotated the pole, making the fist-sized opening wider. "Help me clear this stuff out," Jack directed. He scooped out a few fistfuls of mud. "It's hollow back here."

"And I thought you were going to hit me," AJ joked.

"Not this time," Jack smiled. "Come on. Let's dig this out. Maybe it's the missing link on our map."

⊛ CHAPTER 19 ⊛

Everyone stood waist-deep in the water and pushed the sand, gravel, and larger rocks away to widen the opening. The mud was slimy but packed—tough to break apart.

They dug as fast as they could, and soon the opening was big enough for Kay to squeeze through. She poked her head in.

"Are you really going in there?" Eagle was cautious.

"How else are we going to see what it is?" Kay said. "There's definitely something back there—maybe a passage."

AJ was worried. "Be careful. Just see what it is, then come back."

"I'll be okay. I'm just checking it out." She grabbed her flashlight and slithered through the narrow opening.

"What's it like?" AJ called. "Can you stand?"

From behind the rock wall, Kay flashed her light all around. She was now in a vast cavern, twenty feet wide and as tall as the waterfall. The walls were damp and slippery. A faint light shone in from above. Along the inner wall was a stack of boulders.

"It's a passage!" she shouted. Her voice echoed. "There are boulders that make a staircase. All the way to the top!"

Jack, Eagle, and AJ knelt at the opening, straining to hear her.

"So it is the missing link on the map!" Jack exclaimed. "I guess that's how we're going to get up. Kay was right. They weren't super-human after all." He looked at his friends. "Let's dig it out some more so we all can get through..." Jack hesitated..."with our packs."

"Your pack?" AJ sized Jack up. "You mean big enough for you," he teased.

"Whatever," Jack grumbled.

"Come on. Let's do it," Eagle said. "We can't leave her in there by herself."

The boys dug quickly and then, one by one, pushed themselves through. Kay was waiting for them.

AJ shone his flashlight. "This is incredible! Where's the trail?" His eyes darted all around.

"There!" Kay flashed her light at the boulders stacked along the wall. "It goes that way." Guiding them with her light, she led them up. They were climbing the waterfall from within.

The temperature inside was cooler than on the outside. Water trickled down the walls, and rays of light streamed down from above. The moisture made the rocks slippery. Kay climbed carefully from boulder to boulder. When she reached the top, she pulled herself up and out of the cavern.

She was now on top of the cliff where the water flowed over. She climbed up the ridge to survey the whole area. She could now see that the waterfall that she had just ascended was on offshoot of the main river that cut through a high valley. A large crack in the rock wall surrounding the main river—like a breach in a levee—siphoned off the water that spilled over the cliff. This was the source of the El Gato River. Up here, the water flowed swiftly over boulders, creating whitecaps, before descending the steep slope enroute to their town.

After a few moments, Kay's friends joined her.

"Wow!" Eagle exclaimed. "We made it to the top!"

"Yes." Kay agreed. "And check that out." She pointed away from the river down to a large rock basin off to its side.

From the ridge, with the river behind them, they looked down into a huge bowl-shaped depression, fifty yards deep and fifty feet wide. The walls were rock cliffs that rose hundreds of feet nearly all the way around, except for where they stood. There, the ridge formed a low barrier between the river and the basin below.

On the far side of the huge rock bowl was an enormous manmade wall. It was held together by an intricate network of wood beams and rivets. Wood columns on each side extended up the cliff for a few feet. "What is that?" Eagle marveled. "Way out here somebody built that?"

"Looks like a raised drawbridge to a medieval castle," Kay observed. "Those two columns look like stubby football goal posts. Let's check it out."

While her friends waited on the ridge, Kay climbed down the steep incline to the basin floor. She made her way over to the wooden structure and inspected it. There was a broken plank near the bottom. "What's this?" She poked her head through. A blast of heat hit her face and she pulled back.

AJ followed, descending the basin walls and crossing the flat bottom to Kay. He too inspected the strange structure. It was at least twenty feet high and twenty feet wide. "I don't think it's a drawbridge. Looks to me like a gate."

AJ, too, put his head through the broken plank. "Hey Kay. Did you see there's a gigantic shaft behind here? It's really steep. And whoa! It's hot."

"You said it," Kay agreed.

AJ paused, then shouted. "Hello!" His voice echoed down the shaft. He pulled his head out. He walked over to one of the side columns, pounded on it, and listened. "They're hollow," he concluded.

Kay climbed up some boulders along the back slope of the basin and positioned herself above the gate. She looked down at the side columns. Each one had a round lid a couple yards wide. They looked like big corks. She then studied the cliff above the gate. Grooves were carved into it—like tracks for a garage door. Would it open? she wondered.

Eagle and Jack caught up with them. They were impressed by the scale of the cliffs all around them. Jack had the sensation of being on the field of a huge stadium where the seats rose high into the sky. They walked over to the gate. "It looks solid—and heavy," Eagle remarked.

AJ nodded. "You're right. It's got to weigh a ton."

Kay climbed down the boulders and rejoined her friends.

"This gate must be the smudge that we couldn't make out on the tile," Jack said.

AJ pulled out the old map. "Yes, that got to be it." He looked at the gate.

"This is incredible!" Eagle said.

They all stood mesmerized by the strange sight.

"Did you guys see this?" AJ pointed to the broken wooden plank. "It's glowing down there. I wonder how deep it goes." He put his hands in the opening to gauge the heat. "Rivers of liquid rock must be right down there. Magma. Just like in the mine. But why would there be a manmade gate in front of that crevasse?"

"For safety?" Jack said. "Maybe they didn't want people to fall in." He glared at Kay. "So don't get any ideas."

"Hey, we're headed up to The Spires, not down to the center of the Earth," Kay joked. "We should continue following the trail"—she pointed upward—"before we run out of daylight. We'll figure this thing out later. AJ, where do we go next?"

AJ looked up the steep walls of the basin. "The map says we need to cross the river. The trail picks up again on the other side."

"Let's go that way." Jack pointed toward a gradual slope. "It's the easiest way out of this bowl, and the river's right at the top."

AJ lagged behind his friends as they climbed out. He tried to hide his nervousness. He knew that crossing the river and climbing up to The Spires would be difficult for him. Still, he pressed on, eager to see what lay ahead.

⊛ CHAPTER 20 ⊛

The friends hiked out of the steep basin by using boulders as ladders. They could now see The Spires towering over the valley and Mount Fuego beyond them in the distance.

Jack offered a hand to AJ, pulling him up the last few feet and onto the ridge.

"These cliffs are pretty steep." AJ bent over, trying to catch his breath.

"They are." Eagle agreed. He looked down at the river. "The current here is way too swift. Does the map say where we need to cross?"

AJ knelt down and checked the map. Running between two high ridges, the river cut through solid rock. The swift water created a steep canyon with high walls on either side. However, the lowest point of these walls was where they were standing—right at the edge of the basin. Here the river was flowing only a few yards below them.

"Yes." AJ studied the map. "Down there. Over that ridge." He showed Eagle the markers leading up on the other side of the riverbank.

Kay scrambled up the canyon wall to get a better view. She surveyed the river from above. Downstream, the river narrowed to only a few yards as it approached a sharp turn. Just beyond, a crack in the canyon walls allowed water to exit the main channel. That was the source of the waterfall.

"Do you see a way to cross the river?" AJ asked.

Kay looked past the narrows and the bend. Boulders littered the riverbed. "I think so. We may be able to rock-hop our way across."

AJ shook his head at Eagle. "Did she say rock-hop?"

"I think she did." He laughed. "Something tells me someone's going to get wet."

Kay made her way back down the steep slope to her friends. "We need to get past the narrows. The cliffs end there, and we can get right down to the riverbank. That's where we'll cross."

"Do we have enough time to get to The Spires and make it back to meet Talon?" AJ asked.

Kay checked her phone for the time. "We should be okay," she decided. "Once we get across this river and climb up the other side, the trail is not as steep. Things will move quicker."

The friends climbed up the canyon walls to the top. They walked downstream toward the narrows. The waterfall they had ascended was just off to the side. They jumped over the crack, where the water cascaded down the cliff. They continued past the narrows, and as Kay had described, the canyon walls descended rapidly. They were now at the river's edge. Scattered boulders created white-capped rapids.

"You're right, Kay," AJ said, relieved. "We can cross here."

"I told you," she said. "The current's a little strong, but there are so many rocks, we should be okay. Eagle, do you agree?"

"Absolutely," he said. "Let's start crossing right over there." He led the way down to some boulders right at the river's edge.

Large rocks were close enough together to provide a path. The friends scrambled from rock to rock, being careful not to fall into the swift current. After just a few minutes, they had successfully rock-hopped across.

"See, nobody got wet," Kay said. "Where to, AJ?" she asked.

"Let's go back upstream—across from the basin. That's where the trail picks up."

Kay led the way, climbing up the steep canyon wall on the other side of the river. They followed a path up to a point directly across from the basin and then turned sharply toward The Spires. The trail climbed along a switchback as it gained elevation. They pushed deeper into the rugged terrain as their route led them behind a mountain ridge.

"I can't see The Spires anymore," Eagle said. "Only the cone of Mount Fuego."

"They're on the other side of this peak," Kay explained. "I think we'll see them again when get to the top of this hill."

They were on exposed rock covered with gravel. "Take this slow, AJ," Kay called. "This trail's slippery."

The friends continued to climb up to the last ridge. As

they crested it, they could see The Spires again as well as the entire volcano behind further in the distance.

"There they are!" Kay exclaimed. But quickly her excitement faded. A fifty-foot-wide crevasse blocked their way.

"Darn it!" Kay kicked some dirt. "Does the map show this?" she asked, peeking over the steep edge. The crevasse went down a hundred feet. It circled The Spire ridge on all sides. "This is why no one has been able to get up there," she sighed.

"It's like a moat," Jack noted. "It goes all the way around."

"There's got to be a way across," Eagle said. He made his way over to AJ to study the map. "Where are we?"

AJ pointed to a steep depression on the printout. "The trail follows the ridgeline up"—he paused—"and then it descends rapidly."

"Let me see." Eagle took the map. "Maybe there's a bridge across this thing?"

Jack looked in both directions. "I don't see one, Eagle. The Spires are completely cut off from us—like they're on an island. The gap is too wide even for Kay to get across."

"Well, the map says we have to descend somehow," AJ pointed out. "Let's just go up on this ridge a little more," he suggested. "Maybe we'll see something."

Eagle agreed. "The trail definitely picks up on the other side. We're so close."

They all followed Eagle's lead, keeping the crevasse on their left as they climbed the ridgeline. Every so often Kay would peer over the cliff, gauging the depth of the drop-off.

They continued to climb up to the summit. There, the

ridge they were on veered sharply away from The Spires. There was no bridge or path across that they could see.

"I don't get it," Eagle said. "How can this trail just stop?"

Kay walked over to AJ to study the map. She located their position. "AJ, is this where the trail is supposed to descend?"

AJ nodded. "Right here." He pointed to the edge of the cliff.

Kay and Jack walked up to the spot.

"Jack, grab my belt," Kay directed. "I'm going to lean out over this thing. I want to see if there's anything below us."

"What do you mean?" Jack asked.

"I want get a better view of the ravine we're standing on."

"What are you looking for?"

"I'll let you know when I see it," she replied.

Jack held her firmly by the belt as she got down on her stomach. AJ and Eagle stood next to her. Kay scooted her upper body out over the chasm.

"Well?" Eagle asked. "Do you see anything?"

Kay looked down the near side of the ravine wall. "Hold me tighter, Jack." She stretched farther. "Wait a minute."

"What is it?" AJ asked.

Eagle knelt next to Kay. "Do you see anything?"

"Yes! Pull me up, Jack." Kay pushed back and stood. She looked at her friends. "It's another passage!" she exclaimed. "Cut into the rock right under this lip."

"Another passage?" Eagle marveled.

AJ grew nervous. "How does it lead across that?" He pointed to the ravine. "If it's a tunnel, it's got to be really long." He gulped. "And steep."

"I don't know, but we have to check it out," Kay insisted. "It's got to be the way across—just like the map says. What else could it be? Jack, get the rope."

The opening Kay had spied was ten feet below the top of the ridge. Jack quickly hooked up the rope as Kay put on her harness. Descending backward off the cliff, she rappelled downward, her feet planted on the cliff wall. Within seconds she had entered the small opening. She grabbed her flashlight off her belt and shone it in all directions. She scooted over to the back wall. "There's a shaft here!" she shouted up. She directed her light down the shaft to see what it contained.

AJ yelled back, "Are there steps or just a big chute?"

"Steps. They're wide enough for us to walk down." She paused. "Even for Jack."

"That's a relief." Jack smiled, still holding Kay on the rope.

"Isn't this incredible?" Eagle beamed. " We're almost there. I wish school was this exciting."

The boys laughed.

AJ psyched himself up. "Okay, Jack. I'm ready to do this. Hook me up to the rope. I'm going down to join her."

✦ CHAPTER 21 ✦

One by one they joined Kay at the opening just below the lip of the ridge. Jack lowered AJ and Eagle separately then rappelled himself down. He secured the rope to an anchor so that they could use it later to climb up.

Once they were all in the small cave, Kay directed them to the shaft at the back. "Check out the chisel marks," she said.

AJ felt the sidewalls. He was filled with wonder. "I get it. They used a natural crack in the cliff here and widened it. It must have taken them years to build this place."

"It looks pretty tight." Eagle shone his flashlight down the shaft. "And steep."

"Let's be careful," Jack reminded them. "Let's climb down these steps backwards so we don't fall. Kay, lead the way, and I'll take the rear."

The friends descended within the solid rock as if they were going down a ladder. They used their hands to steady themselves as they carefully placed their feet on the narrow stone steps. Their flashlights shone off the walls, the light bouncing as they descended.

The shaft was just a few feet wider than Jack. His shirt scraped the walls as he climbed down, and he felt his heart race as anxiety welled up. "I don't want to get stuck in here." Closing his eyes and taking deep breaths, Jack paused to collect himself.

"Jack. Are you okay?" Eagle asked. He stopped descending and waited for Jack.

"Yes. I'm good." He exhaled deeply. "Just a little claustrophobic."

"Hold on," Eagle said. "I think we'll get to the bottom soon." Eagle could now see faint light, and it wasn't coming from their flashlights.

"Is that the bottom?" AJ hoped. Like Jack, he was eager to get out of the cramped shaft. He knew that thousands of tons of rock were all around him.

The friends approached the light. One by one they ducked through a narrow crawl space out into the open air. They were now at the base of the crevasse—a hundred feet down. The rock walls above them had tapered like a "V," almost connecting here at the bottom.

Eagle looked up. "Wow! Look how steep it is. Good thing there were steps. Are you feeling a little better, Jack?"

Jack walked across the bottom of the ravine, surveying the other side. "Yeah. Glad that went okay." He took a few deep breaths. "AJ. What does the map say now?"

AJ studied the trail makers. "It says there should be something on this opposite wall. The trail picks up south of here. It's not too far." He led the way.

The friends walked for only fifty yards when AJ stopped. "There! Right there! There's another opening." He pointed about ten feet up on the cliff wall.

"That's got to bring us up to The Spires!" Kay raced over to investigate.

"Kay. Jump up there and see if it's really another passage," Jack directed. "Here, I'll give you a boost." Jack cupped his hands for Kay's foot. He thrust her upward toward the opening. She reached it easily and scrambled up and inside.

"It's another stone staircase," she called down. "There's light in here, too. I hope it goes all the way up to The Spires."

"Let's do this, guys," Jack said. "We only have a few more hours before we need to head back."

Jack boosted AJ and Eagle up to the opening. With a running start, he too cleared the distance. His friends pulled him up and into the passageway.

Inside the cliff, the stairs rose steeply. However, unlike the other shaft, this one had partially caved in. The friends pushed rocks out of their way as they ascended, but doing so became increasingly difficult. They squeezed through the tight shaft, climbing higher within the sold rock. Soon they came to a fork.

"Which way, AJ?" Kay asked.

"I think it's the left one," he replied. "That should lead to the south end of The Spires and the area marked by the gold star on the map."

"But that passageway is dark," Eagle observed. "The light is shining from the other one."

"Let's just go left and follow the map," Kay decided. She

contorted her body around some boulders partially blocking the way, and then continued upward. After a few more yards of climbing she stopped. "There's no way to get through that." She called back to her friends. "We have to take the other shaft—toward the light. This one's completely blocked."

"Well, that stinks," AJ huffed. He stood next to Kay. "The end of the trail and The Spires are through that shaft." He pointed to the blockage. "We're so close. We have to get through."

Kay inspected the cave in. "We're not getting through there," she said bluntly. "We need to take the other passage to the outside and see where it puts us. Jack, head back."

Jack retraced his steps to the fork and followed the light upward. His friends followed. The light became brighter as they ascended. Within a few minutes they were outside.

Jack was the first to emerge. He surveyed the landscape to get his bearings. They were halfway up the cliff, just below the base of The Spires on their north side.

"Can we hike over to the south side from here?" Eagle asked. "That's where we need to be—where the gold star on the map is."

Jack surveyed the overland route to the south end. The terrain was steep and rugged. "What do think, Kay? Can we get there from here?" Jack asked.

Sheer cliffs jutted out from the harsh landscape creating a series of rocky overhangs. It looked like a walled fortress, guarding the south end of The Spires.

"No way." She shook her head. "It's too steep and we'd need to be hanging upside down for most of the climb." She turned and studied the landscape directly above her to the north end.

"But we're so close," AJ said. "There's got to be some way to get there."

"There may be." Kay looked squarely at AJ. "Let's climb up to the north side of The Spires and see what that looks like." She paused. "But, honestly AJ, I don't think you're going to like my answer."

⊛ CHAPTER 22 ⊛

"I can't believe I'm really at The Spires!" Kay beamed. "No one but the Tectonic elders has ever been here. And us! We're the only ones to see this amazing view!"

They were at the base of the outermost rock column on the north side. The Spires rose from a sheer cliff that went down hundreds of feet into a vast valley.

"You're right, Kay. This is amazing." AJ tore himself away from gazing at the spectacular view to study the map. "But we need to be on the south side of these things. That's where the gold star is. Not here. How are we going to get across?"

Eagle went to the edge of the cliff and peered down. "There's no path I can see. Just the sheer rock."

"We'll have to climb out on them sideways—y'know, across their front." Kay took a long look at the rock columns.

"Are you serious?" AJ breathed heavily. He was still panting from the hike up. "How are we going to do that?

There's no ridge to walk on. It looks dangerous."

Kay put her pack down and looked at AJ. "Whatever's on the south side of this thing, the elders went to great lengths to keep it a secret—or at least difficult to reach. The shaft directly to them was blocked. But I can climb across these things and see what's on the other side."

"AJ, this is where the legend talks about unleashing great power," Eagle added. "We're almost there—at its source! We've got to get to the spot marked by the gold star and see what's there."

"Jack, get the rope," Kay directed. "We're not stopping now. I'm going out and over."

AJ removed his pack. He reached for his snack bag and grabbed a granola bar. He then sat on top of his backpack like a chair. Air squeezed out of it as if it were a cushion. He looked at Eagle. "Well, this should be fun to watch, and I'm glad I'm not doing it. It's only a three-hundred-foot drop to a rocky valley," AJ joked. "I say it takes her under five minutes to get across."

"It's going to take her longer than that." With one hand braced against the base of the outermost rock column, Eagle leaned out over the expanse. "I can't even see the other side of The Spires, but I'm not betting against her." He moved back from the precipice and joined AJ by sitting on his own pack. Air squished out as he sat, too. "All I know is that it would take me forever."

"You and me both." AJ smiled.

Kay and Jack assembled their gear, putting on their harnesses and tying their ropes. She reached for some chalk to dry her hands.

"Kay, are you ready? On belay?" Jack asked.

"Belay on," she replied. "I'm ready."

"Climb away," Jack confirmed.

Kay wedged her foot between slender vertical rocks. She brushed off some vegetation so she could insert her anchors and carabiners. "This is going to be more difficult than I thought," she said to Jack. "I need to make sure I do this right."

"Take your time," he replied. "And make sure your anchors are solid."

Kay climbed out onto the first rock column. She pushed across to the second. Securely fastened, she turned to face the sun. She caught the full view of Mount Fuego towering in the distance.

"That volcano is huge!" she exclaimed. "Guys, you've got to see this!"

AJ ignored her excitement over the view. He was too worried about how he was going to get to the other side.

Kay continued on, digging her hands and feet into small cracks. She methodically worked her way from one column to the next, searching for some indication of what was at the end of the trail and marked by the gold star.

Jack let out more rope. From her vantage point, she could now see all of the columns. Above her, the tops of each were at different heights. She leaned back as much as she could to get a better view. A deep groove in one of the columns just a few yards above her caught her eye.

"Jack. I'm going up to check on something." Kay secured another anchor and carabiner. Wedging her feet into a crack, she lunged for a small ledge and grabbed it. After setting a few more anchors, Kay was at the same height as the deep groove.

She examined it. Looking both ways she saw similar holes carved into the columns of rock. Each hole was at a different height creating an arching line across the rock. "That can't be natural," she said aloud.

"What was that?" Jack called.

"There are holes in these spires," she called back. "I think they're hollow."

"Hollow?" Jack was puzzled. He looked up at the huge column of rock. "How could they be hollow?"

Eagle and AJ got up and stood next to Jack. They waited eagerly to hear what Kay had found.

"Did she say hollow?" AJ asked. "That's really weird." Then he called to her. "Do you see anything on the south end?"

Kay looked down and across The Spires to the far side. "Not yet." She spied a ledge next to the outermost column. "Just another second. I'm almost there."

She hovered over the ledge and noticed an opening that cut deep into the cliff. She lowered herself and squeezed her body between two boulders, contorting her shoulders so she could fit. Her legs now on solid ground, she detached herself from the rope and exhaled deeply. "I found it! Yes it's here!" she shouted. "It's an entrance—to another chamber! And guys, there's a shiny gold star the size of dollar coin right here. We found it!" she repeated.

"Can you believe it?" Eagle smiled at AJ. "Another chamber! And gold! My grandfather's gonna be blown away by all of this. AJ, isn't this incredible?"

AJ looked pale. He peered across The Spires and the sheer drop-off to the valley below. He felt queasy. How was he going to get across and into the chamber on the other side?

⊛ CHAPTER 23 ⊛

"**A**J, you can do it," Jack reassured him. "You're actually pretty good at this stuff. Kay's hooked up the ropes. They're secure."

"I know they are. But I'm still afraid." AJ looked down the cliff. The treetops far below looked like soft pillows, but he knew better. "I just don't think I can climb across sideways."

"Maybe you don't have to," Eagle said.

"Oh no?" AJ raised an eyebrow. "You have an idea?"

Eagle looked at Jack. "What if Kay sets up the ropes like Devil's Drop—the amusement park ride. She can loop the rope through the cracks above us"—Eagle pointed—"and we can all swing over."

"Wow—what a great idea. That would work," Jack said. "And she could do that pretty quick, too."

"But remember, I didn't go on Devil's Drop," AJ pointed out.

"That's true." Eagle put his arm around AJ. "But look at it this way. The next time you go to the park, you'll go on it, and it'll be a piece of cake. Close your eyes and you'll be on the other side in no time."

"Okay." AJ psyched himself up. "You're right. I can do this."

"Great." Jack pumped his fist. "Let's get going."

"This really is a devil's drop," AJ laughed nervously.

"Yeah," Eagle affirmed. "It's gonna be lots of fun."

AJ grabbed a harness. "I'll let you know about that once I'm on the other side."

Jack relayed the plan to Kay. She moved high across the rock surface to set up the rope swing. She found a deep crack and secured three separate anchors. She looped the rope through all three, reducing the stress on each point, and then climbed back to the ledge on the far side. Jack still held the rope so he attached it to AJ's harness. The rope swing was secure and ready for action.

"I can't believe I'm doing this," AJ moaned.

"This will work," Jack assured him. "All you have to do is enjoy the ride. Kay's tied off the other end of the rope, and you'll swing like on Devil's Drop all the way across to the other side."

AJ gulped hard.

"Oh, and one more thing," Jack said. "You'll need to take running start to make it across. I'll push you out right at the edge."

"Are you serious?" AJ shook his head. "I've got to jump off this thing—over a three-hundred-foot cliff—with you pushing me?"

"Yeah," Jack said nonchalantly. "It's gonna be great."

AJ looked at Eagle. "Am I the only one here who thinks this is crazy? What if I get stuck out there? What if the rope comes loose?"

"That won't happen and you know it." Eagle paused. "I think." He smiled. "No, seriously. Kay set it up. It's not gonna break. You may dangle out there for a minute or two, but they'll get you at some point," Eagle joked. "Have some faith. It'll be fun!"

AJ hung his head. "Urghh!" he grumbled. He pulled on his harness and tested the buckles about five times to make sure it was secure. The rope was tied to a harness at his waist. He positioned himself ten paces back from the edge of the cliff and clutched the rope with both hands. "Jack, you ready?"

"I'm ready. Are you?" Jack tugged AJ's harness as a final safety check.

AJ took a deep breath and gave a thumb's-up sign.

"Let's do it." Jack returned his signal. "Kay. He's coming across," Jack shouted. He turned to give AJ some last-minute advice. "Okay, just run as fast as you can and jump straight off."

"I can't believe I'm doing this." AJ shook his head. "Eagle, get a picture. No one else is going to believe it either."

"Will do." Eagle reached for his phone.

"On three," Jack called. "Ready? One...Two...Three!"

AJ took one last breath, put his head down and darted toward the edge of the cliff. "*Ahhhhh,*" he screamed as he ran. Just before he reached the edge, Jack pushed him hard into the open air. He soared like a circling hawk, around the rock spires and directly into the view of Mount Fuego. To his surprise, his eyes were open. His hands cramped from clutching the rope and his heart pounded. Time seemed to stand still as he swung closer to Kay on the other side. He twisted on the line and tried to right himself as he approached. He spread his legs and bent his knees to absorb the shock of landing. As his legs struck the ledge, he felt a hard tug on his harness. Kay had grabbed him and pulled him quickly next to her. Dazed, he sank down on his knees. He let out a long breath.

Kay knelt beside him. "You okay?"

AJ's face was white. His heart was still pounding, and he collected his thoughts in silence. His eyes met hers. "That was incredible!" he exclaimed. "Absolutely amazing! I can't believe I just jumped off a cliff." AJ looked out over the expansive valley. He sat down while Kay unhooked him. He was shaking slightly, still feeling the effects of the adrenaline rush. "I think I'm ready for Devil's Drop."

Kay smiled. "Absolutely, AJ." She turned to preparing the rope swing for Eagle. "Absolutely."

⊛ CHAPTER 24 ⊛

Eagle swung across the expanse, and Kay helped him land. He joined AJ inside the chamber. Next Jack sent their packs across. Kay caught them and sent the rope back. Lastly, Jack himself swung across. As Kay was helping him unhook, AJ called.

"Jack, Kay, come in here," AJ shouted. "You've got to see this."

Kay and Jack scampered over jagged rocks toward the opening. They passed the narrow exit of the shaft that led up from below. It was completely blocked off. "I guess going around was our only option," Jack said.

Kay nodded.

As Jack and Kay stood at the cave entrance, they saw thin beams of light shining in through gaps in the ceiling. The cave was deep but not tall. It extended the entire length of the spire columns from the inside. AJ and Eagle were staring at a strange structure. It was built into the rock wall directly behind The Spires.

"Can you believe this place?" AJ marveled.

Several columns of rock rose up from the floor to the ceiling. They were the bottom sections of some of The Spires.

Positioned in front of the middle columns, covered in dust and spider webs, was a manmade device. It was a rectangular stone box about six feet long. In back, metal gears connected to pipes that led into the rock columns.

Eagle surveyed the strange machine and the rock columns behind it. "They look like organ pipes. Like in a church." He walked over to investigate.

"You're right," AJ agreed. "It does look like a pipe organ." He too walked over and used a slender rock to pull back some spider webs to expose more of the machine. "Hey, what's this?"

AJ followed the pipes that went into the middle of the strange device. He noticed that many of them were cracked. They intersected into a rectangular box a foot and a half long. He reached in to clear dirt away. He felt some bumps and ridges. "It's another metal cylinder!" he exclaimed. "Just like the metal key. But this one is much bigger—and wider."

"Another cylinder?" Eagle shone a flashlight inside the box. "Look—it's in pretty bad shape. It's cracked and most of those spikes and ridges are sheared off."

Jack asked, "What do you think it is?"

"I know the rock columns look like organ pipes, but this part looks like an old player piano," Kay declared. "Right, AJ? A metal cylinder would spin in the middle, playing a pre-set tune."

AJ nodded. "You're right! But this thing isn't playing anything. It needs serious repairs."

Kay turned her attention to the other walls. "This place is unbelievable." The rays of light illuminated a mural on the wall. She walked closer to get a better look. "And look at this! That's the same style as in the mine. That's Mount Fuego. It's erupting." She ran her hand over the mural, brushing off dust. "And that's the lava flow off the north side." She wiped her forehead with her sleeve. "Man, it's hot in here."

Eagle joined Kay. He grabbed a bandana from his pocket and soaked it with water from a water bottle. He cleaned the surface of the mural. "Hey, is that the path we took to get up here? The waterfall. The basin with the gate. And the river."

"You're right," Kay agreed. "But what's that in the river?"

Kay shone her flashlight to see the mural more clearly. The river was dammed up where the cliffs narrowed. Water was overflowing, and filling the basin. "Hey, Eagle—look—the gate's up on its tracks." Kay called AJ over. "What's happening here, AJ? Is water flowing under the raised gate? Remember, it was super hot back there."

"Yes." He studied the mural. "I wonder how deep that shaft goes?"

"What are you thinking?" Eagle asked.

"Well, the Tectonic legend tells us how they could release a great power to reshape the Earth. If that shaft beyond the gate goes deep—I mean really deep, like when they drill for gas—then all that water going into the Earth could do something dramatic."

Jack was confused. "I don't understand. Where are you going with this?"

"Well, that's what fracking is," AJ explained. "Gas companies inject tons of water into the ground to break up the rock and release the trapped gas. I just read that the water they force down into the Earth can actually cause earthquakes."

"Seriously?" Kay said.

"Yes!" AJ said. "It's all over the news. It can shift the rock beds and make them slide."

"That sounds bad," Eagle said.

"Yes," AJ agreed. "But here, maybe that type of power could open up a crack in the bedrock on the north slope." He considered the mural that showed the lava flow. "That would reduce the pressure under the cone of the volcano and prevent the top of the mountain from blowing off. Then the lava would flow harmlessly out the side where nobody lives. Maybe that's what happened hundreds of years ago when the Tectonic were still around."

Jack walked back to the ancient machine. "Okay. Let's just say for the moment that somehow water goes into the basin, goes down that shaft behind the gate, and causes the volcano to release the lava safely on its north slope." He looked skeptical. "Then what is this thing for?"

AJ looked skeptical, too. "Well for water to get down the shaft with enough force, the gate would have to be out of the way. What does that? This machine and the gate seem too far apart to be directly connected." He paused. "But it's got to do something. Why else would it be here?"

"If we could get it to work, then we'd know for sure what it does," Kay pointed out.

Eagle inspected the machine. He touched one of the

columns in back that rose to the ceiling. "They really do look like pipes from a church organ. Do you think these can make sounds? I don't see any holes."

"Like a song of the mountain?" Jack smiled. "How's it supposed to do that?"

"These columns are definitely hollow," Kay asserted. "I could see the holes from outside when I went across them."

AJ concentrated on the ancient contraption. "A player piano and pipe organ," he mused. He envisioned that when the cylinder spun, the gears moved up and down, opening the pipes. "If it were designed to create tones, it would need to run on something." He paused. "Maybe steam?"

"Steam?" Eagle asked. He scanned the room, wiping the sweat off his brow. "But where would that come from?"

"I don't know," AJ replied. "But forcing steam through these pipes would definitely make a sound. A really big one! Like a factory whistle or gigantic tea kettle."

"Well, it is really hot in here—and sticky," Kay said. "Maybe there's a lever or something that turns the machine on." She brushed back layers of spider webs. "Fan out. Let's see if we can find it."

The friends spread through the room. Eagle followed the pipes and gears along the back wall to where they intersected with the ground. Poking through the dirt was the rim of a wheel valve. "Over here. I found something!" Eagle called.

Kay ran over and knelt next to him. They brushed away dirt and cobwebs until the wheel was fully exposed. Figuring it would be difficult to turn, she called to Jack. "You're up, big guy."

"Hold on!" AJ interjected. "Should we turn that thing?

We don't know what it does."

Kay stepped back, giving Jack some room. "We've got to risk it. We've come this far. Let's see what happens. Jack, get ready to turn it off if we need to."

Jack flexed his bicep and moved into position. Reaching down, he grabbed the circular valve. It was the size of a steering wheel. "This looks like something you'd find on a submarine hatch."

"Turn it, Jack," Eagle said eagerly.

Jack applied pressure. He strained and felt it give. He turned it one full rotation. Instantly the chamber shook and gurgled.

"That doesn't sound good." AJ scanned the room. The noise and shaking intensified. The cylinder knocked against the gears, stuck in its housing. It was trying to spin. Suddenly thick vapor rose from cracks in the pipes along the back wall. The chamber filled with steam.

"Jack!" Eagle shouted. "Turn it off! Turn it off!"

Jack grabbed the wheel and pulled it back around. The noise and shaking stopped, although steam hung in the air.

AJ studied a cracked pipe next to the broken metal cylinder at the base of the machine. "So I think I was right." He peered into the device. "Steam spins the cylinder, but some of these pipes channeling the steam to it are cracked. From there, it looks like the cylinder directs steam to the rock columns above." AJ was proud of himself. "But here's the problem—or at least one of them. If we want to get this thing to work, we'll need to patch all these holes." AJ ran his hand along the cracks. He re-inspected the broken cylinder and frowned.

"What's the problem, AJ?" Kay asked. "Can't you fix that?"

"I can fix the pipes, but not this cylinder."

"So let me get this straight," Eagle said. "The ancient Tectonic legend talks about how they were able to reshape the land by using a powerful device. We've found their map and this mysterious device designed to do something big— one would think. Here it is." He pointed to the machine. "But you're telling us it's too broken and we can't fix it?" Eagle paused for dramatic effect. "We've got to get this thing to work!"

"AJ, you can fix it, right?" Jack asked. "You can fix everything."

"I can fix the broken pipes and gears, but I have no idea how to fix the cylinder. I'd need to know the length of each spike. Believe me, I wish I could fix it, really. But if it's supposed to direct the steam to a specific rock column, I'd need to copy the original pattern from somewhere."

There was a long silence.

"Wait." Kay got AJ's attention. "What if you had the original mold—y'know, to make this cylinder?" She pointed to the broken object. "Then we could recreate it perfectly— an exact match. Right?"

"Sure, but where are we going to get..." AJ cut himself off. He stared back at Kay. She was grinning. He shook his head. "No, you can't be serious."

"What's going on?" Jack asked. "What are you guys talking about? Do you guys have the original mold?"

Seconds later, Eagle's eyes lit up. He, too, grinned. "Yes, yes, Jack!" He could hardly contain his excitement. "We do!"

CHAPTER 25

"You want to do *what*?" Jack asked in disbelief.

They were heading down the mountain. It was a long way back and they needed to make good time to get to Talon's before dark.

"Seriously?! You want to go back into the mine? You were almost cooked in there the last time. Why would you want to do that?"

"I know it's crazy, but there was another mold in there. It was bigger and heavier than the one we took out— and much wider. It looked like it would make a cylinder that would fit in the machine up there." Eagle showed Jack the picture that AJ had taken in the mine. "This was in the small chamber where AJ got the first one that made the cylinder key. Right, AJ?"

AJ nodded and flashed a weak smile. "I remember it being the right size." He was nervous. "But like Jack said, we almost got cooked."

"We'll figure something out," Kay said calmly. "Right now we just need to meet Talon and have his chili. Then we can think about how to get back in the mine."

"I agree," Eagle said. "It might still be too hot—but maybe it's not. Who knows? We'll just have to see."

Jack gave Eagle a skeptical look. "Okay, let's go get that chili. We'll check out the mine tomorrow."

The four friends continued down the mountain. They knew that Talon was going to be amazed by their discoveries.

* * * * * *

The next day the four friends went back to the mine. They climbed up to the top of the mound and stood over the airshaft, the site of their narrow escape. Their discovery was still a secret, helped by the fact that the rock formation was far from town and a mile from the nearest road.

"You guys crawled through that?" Jack considered the narrow entrance. "I'm not going to fit through there."

"I can't believe this was your idea, AJ," Eagle said. "You really want to go back in?"

"No," AJ replied. "This was Kay's idea. But the mold is probably in there. If we want to get the machine to work, we have to get the mold."

"This is craziness." Jack shook his head. "We don't even know how that machine would work or what it would do."

"Look," Kay snapped. "At this point we're just going to see if we can safely enter the mine. If we can—and only if we can—we'll try to get that mold out. The fate of our town may be in our hands. If we can fix the machine and it works as the legend says, we won't have to leave. Everyone will be saved.

We need to at least try."

They all thought over Kay's words.

"I guess if we have to go in there, you'll make it safe." AJ looked over to Kay. "Right?"

"What was that?" Kay smiled, pretending she didn't hear. She was unfurling her climbing rope on a tarp and organizing her protection equipment.

"Very funny," AJ smiled.

Eagle leaned over the vent. Warm spray hit his face. He heard a low gurgle from below.

Jack held his hand over the vent, too. "It's hot, but not scalding. That's good. Right?" He noticed pebbles dancing around the opening. Intrigued, he leaned in closer. Loose rocks start to slide down the mound.

"Jack, move back!" AJ shouted.

Startled, Jack quickly moved away. Suddenly, a shrill sound rang out. Steam shot from the vent. Knocked off balance, Jack slid down the hillside headfirst. He righted himself and frowned. His face was covered in dirt. "This could be a problem."

Warm water rained down as they retreated from the mound.

"Looks like this isn't going to happen," Kay said. "This geyser's still pretty active."

"It is." AJ kicked some loose stones in disappointment. "But I wonder..." He cut himself off. "Maybe we still can do it." AJ had a knowing glint in his eye. "Kay. What time is it?"

"Around eight-thirty. Why?"

"No, exactly," AJ pressed. "What's the exact time?"

Kay looked at her phone. "It's 8:35. Why?" she repeated.

AJ held up both hands. "Okay." He started to talk fast. "I have an idea—and I can't believe I'm suggesting this—but let's just wait and see how long it takes to erupt again."

"AJ, what are you thinking?" Eagle asked.

"Well, I did this report about geysers at Yellowstone last year, and many of them erupt on a regular cycle. It has to do with the time it takes for the water to heat up and get pressurized. If this geyser has a regular cycle, then maybe we can enter when it's recharging. If it's not too hot, that is."

Jack laughed. "AJ, you're crazy. You think you can still go in there?"

"Yes, I'm totally serious," AJ replied. "When we were in there before, most of the heat and steam vented through this airshaft. That made it bearable. Plus, if the cycle's regular, it'd be safe. It may take hours or even days to get hot again. If that's true, we'd have plenty of time to get in and out before anything happened. Let's just hang out and see. I brought some snacks."

"Snacks?" Jack moved in closer. He wiped the dirt off his hands and face and grabbed the pack. "What'd ya bring?"

They all waited, eating granola bars and sipping water. Every half hour AJ climbed the mound and held his hand over the vent. The air coming out was only lukewarm. Lounging in the sun, they waited patiently to see if the geyser would erupt again. Around noon, AJ noticed pebbles sliding down the mound. The friends all ran up to the vent. AJ put his hand over it and pulled it back quickly.

"Move down," he directed. "Kay. What's the time?"

"12:10."

They all retreated from the opening as large rocks

jiggled loose. Then steam erupted again with the same piercing whistle.

"Man, that's loud!" Eagle covered his ears.

Once again, warm droplets rained down. Kay wiped the glass face of her phone with her sleeve. "Now what?"

"Let's see what happens around 3:30. Maybe it's about a three-and-a-half-hour cycle."

"We have to wait here another three hours?" Jack complained. "I need lunch."

"Why don't you grab us all something from Fiery Bill's?" Kay suggested. "We need to make sure this thing is safe and stable if we are going to have any chance of going in."

"That works for me." Jack jumped to his feet. He trotted down the mound to his bike and rode off toward town.

Kay, Eagle, and AJ sat and pondered their situation. Could they really get back into the mine? Would the mold make another cylinder to replace the broken one? If it fit into the machine, what would it do?

"I hope it's not too dark by the time we figure this thing out," Eagle said, crunching another granola bar.

"As long as it's a regular cycle, we can always come back tomorrow. We just need to be sure."

"Do you really think we can fix the machine with what's in there?" Eagle asked.

"If it's the cast for the broken piece of that machine, then absolutely," AJ replied.

"Well, I'm not eating any more chicken wings to get this one made," Eagle declared bluntly. "My stomach hurt for days."

They all laughed.

"I think we'll be okay," AJ assured him. "I talked to my friend last night and he said that the Big Fish is on vacation. He'll just make the metal piece for us—that is, if we can get the mold to him."

"That's a relief," Eagle smiled.

Jack returned about an hour later, and they sat eating their BBQ, waiting for something to happen. Sure enough, at around three-thirty, the ground shook. A few minutes after that, the geyser erupted.

"You really are a science genius, AJ," Jack said. "I can't relate." They all giggled.

AJ looked proud. "Well, let's wait another cycle or two— to be sure. But it looks like this could work. We'll have a little over three hours. That will be the window. That should give us enough time. Zip in. Zip out. Right?"

"Yes," Kay nodded. "That'll work."

⬡ CHAPTER 26 ⬡

The next day they were back at the mine. They had spent the previous day timing the cycle of the eruptions. It was regular, lasting a little over three hours.

Kay organized her gear. It was just after nine in the morning, and the geyser was about to blow. Kay and Jack had set up all the climbing equipment, anchoring the protection for the ropes around large boulders. Both she and Eagle had harnesses around their waist and legs, and they were prepared to lower themselves through the small opening.

"Okay, here's the setup." AJ pulled out a diagram so they all could see. "Kay will go down into the mine and Jack will hold the rope for her. Eagle will also go in and I'll hold the rope for him. Eagle, you'll need to relay commands to Kay, since she'll be deep in there on the other side of this airshaft."

Eagle nodded.

AJ continued. "Kay will also take an extra rope tied to

her back and this duffel bag." He held it up. "When she gets to the small chamber on the far side, she'll place one half of the mold in the bag, and then Jack will pull it out. Both halves are too heavy to go out at one time. Now this is important." He made sure everyone was listening. "Kay won't be able to climb while Jack's pulling the bag out. She'll just have to stay put. After Jack pulls out the bag with the first mold, he'll send the bag back down to Eagle, and he'll throw it over to Kay for her to load up the second mold. After Jack pulls out both halves, he'll hook himself back up to Kay. I'll pull Eagle out first and then Kay will follow. Sound good?"

"Did it take you all night to come up with that?" Kay asked cheerfully. "What could go wrong?" She looked at Jack to see if he was on board.

"You mean with this insane plan?" Jack rolled his eyes. "Y'know, Dad would kill us if he knew we were doing this."

"I know. But we'll be safe. And if things don't look right down there, I'm just going to leave," Kay promised.

"That's right," Jack said sternly. "At the first sign of trouble, if you think that geyser's going to erupt, I'm pulling you out. Got it?"

"This will work, Jack," Kay assured him. She placed her hand over the vent. "Anyway, it's not nearly as hot as it was when we were in there last time. We'll have more than three hours, and like you said, if things don't look right, I'll get out."

"I'll make sure the ropes are secure," AJ said.

"Zip in, zip out," Jack instructed Kay. "Don't waste time. Just to be sure, when two hours are up, you're out. Got it?"

Kay nodded. "That gives us plenty of time to be safe. You okay with that, Eagle?"

He looked pale. "Umm. Okay." He hesitated.

"Are you having second thoughts about going in?" Kay asked.

"Yes, but I'm good." He clenched his fist to psyche himself up. "Let's do it."

Kay stood off to the side of the geyser opening. Rocks moved all around her feet and then the warm vapor shot out from the shaft.

"It's like a natural shower!" Jack observed. "I should have brought some shampoo," he joked. "Good thing it's not too hot."

After waiting for about ten minutes for the geyser to end and the vent to cool, Kay scrambled up to the opening. She tested the heat and then pulled her harness snug around her waist.

"On belay?" she asked Jack, double-checking that he had her securely roped in.

"The belay is on," he confirmed. "Climb away."

Kay attached her headlamp, gripped the rope, and stepped backward into the shaft. She pressed her feet against the sidewalls as she lowered herself into the chamber.

"You're up, Eagle," AJ called. "I've got you." He threaded the rope though his safety belay and secured it to himself. The D-shaped carabiner clicked shut. "Just follow her down. If there's a problem, yell, and I'll pull you out."

"Sounds easy," Eagle joked. "Okay, here I go." He slid down into the shaft.

The cramped vent was hot but not overwhelmingly so. Kay and Eagle lowered themselves quickly into the chamber. They both dangled just underneath the ceiling. The glow was intense, as a stream of molten lava still bubbled where the stone cauldron had hung. A dense fog obscured their vision. Water now poured in from the crack in the sidewall, flowing down into the opening in the floor. The sizzle from the water hitting the magma underneath was an eerie reminder of their previous visit.

Kay reached for protection equipment from her harness belt. She was ready to traverse the ceiling to the opening of the smaller chamber. "Eagle. Just wait here like we planned." Kay spied a crack in the ceiling in which to insert her anchor. She found a piece that was the right size and calmly wedged it into the rock. She tugged on it, making sure it was secure. She clipped a carabiner clasp to its end and pulled her rope through it so that she could suspend herself from that spot. She repeated this process three more times as she moved upside down across the ceiling to the opening at the far end.

"Kay," Eagle called. "You're amazing! I wish I had video of this. You'd get a million hits. You have your phone, right?"

"I have it." She looked at the time. She was making good progress across the ceiling. "One more anchor and I'll be set." She reached for it and methodically secured it in place. "Eagle. Tell Jack to give me a little slack. I'm going to try and swing into the chamber."

Eagle relayed the instructions. Kay hovered near the small entrance and swung her feet forward. She cleared the sill and crouched down. She was now on solid ground.

"Slack!" she shouted, tugging on the rope.

"Give her more slack," Eagle yelled. "She's in."

Jack let out the rope, and Kay was able to move into the tight passageway. Her headlamp lit the way. The passageway opened up into a small, hot room. She ducked in and looked around.

"Do you see them?" Eagle called. "The two halves?"

Kay tilted her head to swivel her lamp. In the corner she spied a pair of rocks propped against the wall. "I found them!" She moved in closer.

She spread the duffel bag on the ground. She reached for one half of the stone mold, grabbing it with both hands. Bending her knees, she wedged her hands under it and lifted to test the weight. The piece was heavy—around forty pounds. She rolled it into the duffel. She zipped it up and attached the handle to a carabiner. She yanked it to test whether it was secure and then called to Eagle, "Pull it up!" She dragged the heavy bag to the entrance and pushed it off the ledge. She watched it swing over the open space as Jack hoisted it out of the chamber from above.

Meanwhile, Jack was tugging hard on the rope. He had looped it around a boulder to give himself more leverage. Fist over fist, he pulled. Below, once the bag had ascended, Eagle positioned it under the narrow airshaft. It was just wide enough for the bag to fit through without getting stuck. Within a few moments Jack and AJ saw the bag emerge from the vent. With AJ's help, Jack secured the bag, removed the stone mold, and sent the bag back down to Eagle as planned.

"Eagle, here you go," Jack called. "Send this back over to Kay."

"Got it," Eagle replied. He grabbed the bag and threw it over.

"Just like the carnival games," she smiled. Kay disappeared from his view as she went to collect the second piece. Moments later she returned, carrying the heavy bag. She swung it over the ledge and into the misty chamber and, as before, she watched it rise as Jack pulled it out. Everything was going according to plan.

"We'll be out of here soon," Eagle called to Kay. He looked down at the floor of the chamber. "It looks like it's starting to get hot again."

Kay checked her phone. She was surprised that almost two hours had passed. "Yep, it's time to go," she called back. "Does Jack have me hooked up yet? I can't go anywhere till he does."

"Just another second." Eagle looked into the vent above him. He could see the duffel bag clear the opening to the outside.

Topside, Jack quickly recovered the duffel bag, then retied himself on the rope to hold Kay. Within seconds, he was ready. "The belay is on, Kay. Climb away!"

"He's ready, Kay," Eagle relayed. "Come back across."

Kay stood at the edge of the small entrance to the secondary chamber. She peered down at the floor with its channel of molten rock. The room glowed from the heat, and a dense fog was settling in. "Eagle, get out of here. I'm right behind you."

Eagle hesitated briefly, then called up to AJ. "I'm coming out. AJ, take up the rope." Eagle shimmied up.

Kay leaped up to a handhold in the ceiling. She retraced her route, removing the equipment she had placed earlier and clipping each anchor to loops on her harness. Within minutes she had arrived at the airshaft that led out. She looked up through it and saw Eagle's silhouette almost at the exit. She prepared to head up, but then she stopped. She touched the walls, feeling for a vibration. There was none. She checked her phone. "I still have some time," she muttered. "Jack, give me some slack!" she yelled up.

"Slack?" he shouted.

"Yes." She demanded. "Do it now!"

Jack released some rope so Kay could maneuver. He was confused. Why would she need more rope to head out?

Kay had lowered herself to just under the opening of the airshaft. Thick steam was all around her. She heard popping and bubbling twenty feet below. The water was starting to bubble up. She felt the smooth sidewalls through the dense fog. Then her hand struck something firm. "There it is!" she exclaimed. She moved closer to the sidewall and hovered next to the shiny silver icicle she had lodged there a few days earlier. She grabbed it with both hands and tried to jiggle it loose.

Jack started to worry. "What's she doing?" He looked at AJ. "I'm pulling her out." He took up the rope. "We don't have a lot of time."

The rope pulled tight on Kay's harness as she was lifted from her position. She clung to the silver shard, her body stretching between it and the rope.

"Jack, stop!" she protested. "Give me ten seconds. There's still time. I know what I'm doing." Reluctantly, Jack released some slack.

Steam had now completely filled the chamber. It was hard for her to see. She still clung to the silver spike stuck in the wall. She yanked. Her eyes lit up as it moved slightly. "A few more tugs," she thought. "Just a few more."

Now the chamber started to tremble. She knew time was running out. The geyser was going to blow soon.

"Her time is up," Jack said, flatly. "I'm getting her out of there. Guys"—he directed—"pull up that rope!"

Kay almost had the silver spike free. She was determined to give one more pull; then she would scramble out. She knew it would take her only a few seconds to exit. She also knew that the steam was not quite ready to erupt. She had been in this exact spot before.

Preparing for one last pull, she grabbed the spike with both hands. Suddenly her entire body was propelled upwards by her harness. Jack was pulling her up. The jolt yanked the silver spike free from the wall! She clutched it in her hand. Surprised but gleeful, she righted herself and made a beeline for the exit. She moved swiftly, her legs darting from side to side as she raced upward.

Jack, Eagle, and AJ picked up the slack feverishly. The rocks on the ground shook all around them.

"If she makes it out of there, I swear I'm gonna kill her." Jack pulled frantically.

A split second later, Kay poked her head out of the hole and threw herself onto the ground. She rolled a few feet down the slope. When she halted, she looked up at the opening where her friends stood staring at her. She was covered in dirt from head to toe.

"Hey," she said calmly. "Everyone good here?" She exhaled deeply, turning so no one could see. "I knew I had plenty of time."

Seconds later, the geyser shot out with a boom, and warm droplets rained down. Kay smiled and held up the six-inch solid silver spike. "I had to go back and get this. It's a good luck charm. And check out how cool it is. It sparkles." She twisted it so they all could see.

"Kay, you're crazy!" Jack shook his head. "You went back for that?"

"Absolutely crazy!" Eagle helped her up.

She laughed, blushing slightly. "Yeah, I guess I am."

⊛ CHAPTER 27 ⊛

"**K**ay, get up!" Jack pushed opened her bedroom door. "Didn't you feel that quake?"

Kay squinted, trying to adjust her blurred vision. "I didn't feel anything. I was sleeping."

"Well, they're getting bigger," Jack said. "I just saw on the news that they're going to make a decision on the evacuation soon. The pressure under the mountain is building up faster than they expected."

Kay flopped back onto her pillow.

"Did you hear what I said?" Jack jostled her. The whole bed rocked.

"I'm up. I'm up," she groaned.

"Good. Eagle and AJ are coming over. We need to get an early start today. We have a lot to do. AJ's friend made the new cylinder late last night. He said it looks good. Once they get here, we'll head up to the mountains."

"Okay." Kay pushed back her covers. "Get out. I'll be ready in a few."

While Kay was getting ready, AJ and Eagle rode up on their bikes. AJ had with him his makeshift wagon carrier attached to his bicycle. He used it when he needed to haul heavy objects around town.

Jack met them on the driveway. "She'll be out in a second. She just got up."

AJ showed Jack the newly-forged cylinder which he had fastened in the wagon. It had the same shape as a rolled-up yoga mat, but it was solid. Metal spikes of different lengths stuck out over its surface.

Jack tested its weight. "Not bad—Thirty pounds?"

"That's about right," AJ confirmed. "You should be able to fit it into your backpack. Right?"

"Sure. We'll just need to wrap it so I don't get poked. What's all this other stuff?" Jack asked.

"We'll need it to fix the machine," AJ replied. "PVC pipe, a few tools. The basics. I've taken just what we need to fit in our backpacks."

Moments later, Kay joined everyone on the driveway. She had her ropes and climbing gear. She opened her pack and inserted the silver icicle she had retrieved from the mine the previous day.

"You really need that?" AJ asked. "Isn't it heavy?"

"It's not too bad," she replied. "It'll be good for digging out the opening under the waterfall—like a pickaxe. We'll need something to help us widen it so Jack can fit through with that cylinder." She held the silver icicle up to the light. "Plus, it's my new good luck charm." She loaded the remaining gear into her backpack, making sure it was balanced. "You guys ready?"

"Ready? We've been waiting on you." Jack rolled his eyes.

"Great!" Kay ignored him. "Let's head off."

The friends started their bike ride toward the mountains. They were curious and excited, wondering if the machine would really work. If so, what would it do? They arrived at the trailhead and stowed their bikes. They consolidated their gear and headed up, following the same path they had taken a few days earlier. Making good time, they arrived at the cave behind the waterfall. As Kay had predicted, mud had already filled in the opening to the passage on the back wall of the cave. Kay reached into her backpack and pulled out the silver icicle. She plunged it into the soil, loosening it up so the others could scoop it out.

"It is useful," AJ admitted.

After a few minutes of digging, the opening was wide enough for Jack to fit through, even with his large pack. One by one, they crawled into the hidden passageway and up the inside of the cliff. The cascading water clamored outside.

Soon they exited the passage and stood on the perch next to the river. It flowed swiftly beneath them and then over the waterfall that they had just ascended from the inside. Careful not to slip on the wet rocks, they gazed out over the basin and marveled at the wood gate at its far end.

"I still don't get how that thing opens," Jack said. "It must weigh a ton."

"And there's no lever or anything," Eagle added.

"It was definitely open in the mural up at The Spires,"

Kay said. "But I've got to agree with Jack. How does it open?"

AJ chimed in. "Guys, who knows? We're following a legend that's like five hundred years old. Right now we just need to see if the cylinder Jack's carrying fits into the machine. Let's get there, get it working, and then we'll worry about the gate later."

Kay put her arm around AJ. "He's right. We still have to get up to The Spires and swing into the chamber. That's going to take some time. We should get going."

AJ gulped hard. "Oh yeah, swing across The Spires," he muttered. "I can't believe I have to do that again."

The friends soldiered on, rock-hopping across the river and the boulder field and up to the hidden staircase that led into the ravine. One by one they lowered themselves to the cavern under the lip of the ridge and descended. They continued up the other side to the north side of The Spires. On their last visit, Kay had left the ropes attached, so their swing across was much quicker this time. After successfully navigating this last obstacle, they were back in the hidden chamber behind The Spires. AJ was now organizing their gear on the floor, preparing to begin his repairs.

"I'll need to get behind this thing." AJ pointed to the machine. "Those levers and pipes need work." He sucked in his chest and turned his body sideways to fit into the narrow space. He inspected the machine's inner workings. He used a rag to pull back thick layers of cobwebs to reach the broken cylinder. "I've got to get this old thing out." He grabbed it by the spikes and tried to dislodge it.

Jack moved to the front of the machine and held the other end of the cylinder. He jiggled it back and forth. "Geeze," he exhaled. "That's really in there." Sweat ran into his eyes as he strained.

"Hand me a wrench," AJ directed. "I think I can push it out from back here."

Jack grabbed the biggest one. He threaded it through to AJ who was still wedged in behind the machine. AJ stuck the wrench behind the cylinder and pushed it forward until—*pop!* It was free. Jack grabbed it and put in on the floor.

Kay walked over to Jack's backpack. She pulled out the newly created cylinder and compared it with the one they had just removed from the machine. She smiled confidently. "Yep. It's gonna fit."

Still behind the machine, AJ inspected the other gears and levers all around the now empty space. He felt a bracket that had broken off—"That'll need to be fixed," he muttered, then wriggled out to join the others.

"You look like a coal miner," Eagle laughed. "You're completely covered in soot."

"I know." AJ used a rag to wipe his hands and face.

"So what's it look like in there?"

"It' dirty," AJ said wryly. "Lots of spider webs." He brushed himself off.

"I meant the machine," Eagle clarified.

"Oh," AJ smiled. "Well there are some broken gears and pipes, but for the most part, it looks okay. It's going to take me a little time, but I'll get it working." AJ was confident.

They all helped. Eagle and Kay cut sections of PVC tubing. Jack cleaned off the gears and the insides of the old pipes as best he could. Slowly the ancient machine was being restored. By midday, they were ready to test it.

"Okay, Jack," AJ called. "Get ready to turn it on just like you did before."

Jack reached for the wheel gear on the floor next to the machine. He slowly turned it one rotation. The chamber started to rumble. Suddenly vapor spewed from one of the pipes.

"Turn it off," AJ directed. He located the hole. He rifled through his backpack and pulled out some plumbing supplies. He sized them up, and selected a rubber seal and clamp and patched the broken pipe. He called back to Jack, "Try it again."

Once again Jack turned on the steam. The chamber shook again. They all heard water sputtering from underneath. AJ pinpointed the spot and Jack turned off the steam. AJ patched that cracked pipe, too.

After a few more starts and stops, AJ flashed a thumb's-up sign to Jack. "I think I got them all," he said. "Try it now."

Jack turned the valve. The chamber rumbled. Gurgling echoed everywhere, then turned into a low hum. They all watched in amazement as the gears of the machine came to life.

⊛ CHAPTER 28 ⊛

"**W**e did it!" They all cheered as they congratulated themselves.

The cylinder was starting to spin.

"It's working!" Jack exulted. "It's really working!"

"Yes, but it's not doing anything." Kay studied the machine. "AJ, why is it spinning so slow?"

AJ craned his neck to see if the pipes were channeling the steam up the rock columns in back. "Wait a minute." He reached his arm behind the front panel. He felt the flow of air and steam on his hand. "I don't think there's enough pressure in there. The steam's not getting to the columns."

"Can you increase the pressure?" Eagle asked.

"That comes from underground," AJ said bluntly. "Maybe there's a ruptured pipe that we're not seeing." AJ put his hand next to the spinning cylinder.

"Are you kidding me?" Jack sighed. "I can't believe we've

come this far, got this thing to actually work"—he paused—"and it doesn't work!"

"The pressure's just not high enough," AJ said. He inspected his patches on the pipes.

Kay walked over. She put her arm around AJ. "Maybe you can still fix it. Don't give up."

"I guess." AJ slumped. He slithered under the machine to see if he could locate the problem.

Jack went over to its front. As he was peering into a small crack just above the spinning cylinder, something caught his eye. He turned on his headlamp. He bent over to get a closer look. "There's something in there. Maybe it's a blockage." He reached for a stick and poked it into the crack. "Wait. It's moving."

"What's moving?" Eagle drew closer.

Jack kept poking. Suddenly he dropped the stick and fell backward. "It's a—a—" he stammered. He scrambled to his feet and bolted toward the exit. "It's a—tarantula!"

A small brown tarantula poked out of the hole. Its hairy body and legs scuttled across the floor.

Eagle laughed and hustled over to grab the critter. He held it up safely by its abdomen. "Seems harmless." He smiled. "Jack, I don't think this little thing is blocking the steam."

Kay ran over laughing. "Pretty cool." She inspected the spider in Eagle's hand. "Jack, you're such a baby."

"You're crazy for touching that thing, Eagle. Crazy." Jack kept his distance. "Put it down." Jack cowered at the exit. "And Kay, you move away from it, too. You're both freakin' me out."

"It's no big deal, Jack. Really." Eagle dangled the

tarantula in Jack's direction. "They're harmless—if you know how to handle them." Not wanting to unnerve Jack any more, he tossed the spider to the far side of the room.

Jack kept a keen eye on the critter as it made it way toward the wall.

AJ continued to study the inner workings of the device. He tapped the pipes to make sure they were hollow and jiggled the levers to see if they could move freely. "This thing really is amazing." He watched the gears move and listened intently to the airflow as it spun the cylinder.

"Guys." Jack called softly from the entrance to the chamber. He was having trouble projecting his voice. "Guys," he repeated. He was unable to get their attention. Then, with all the energy he could muster, he yelled at the top of his lungs. "Guys!"

Eagle turned. "What?"

Jack's face was white. He pointed behind Eagle. Out of the corner of his eye, Eagle caught sight of Kay cautiously retreating. He then turned back to face the opening above the spinning cylinder. The opening appeared to move. Confused, he focused his eyes. Then his jaw dropped.

"AJ, get out from under there!" Eagle screamed. "Now!" Eagle grabbed him by the shoulder and lifted him toward the exit.

Bewildered, AJ stumbled. He struggled to regain his balance. "What's wrong?" Then his eyes grew wide. Hundreds of spiders poured out from behind the front panel.

"*Ahhh!*" AJ bolted. "The steam." He struggled to catch his breath. "The steam! Their nest must be in there—blocking up the pipes." Keeping his wits, he grabbed the pack lying on the ground as he made his way toward the exit. "Oh my God! I can't believe I was under there!" he screamed as he ran.

"Eagle, they're on your legs!" Kay shouted. She hustled to collect all her gear from the middle of the room. "Get out!" she shouted. The swarm of spiders headed her way. Realizing time was running out, she grabbed as much as she could and ran toward Jack.

Eagle swatted the spiders off his body at a frantic pace. They were pouring out in huge numbers right onto him, more than he had ever seen. He sprang through open patches on the ground. He was careful not to crush any spiders under his feet. The floor appeared to move like a wave as he focused on his escape.

"Run!" Kay yelled again. "Get out!" She felt helpless, watching Eagle fend off the mass of critters by himself. But she was also amazed that he was not completely freaking out.

Eagle leaped to safety. He even managed to grab the remaining gear on his way out. He shivered as he rejoined the others just outside the chamber.

"*Whooo!*" Eagle exhaled. "Look at all of them." Eagle brushed his body. "I can take one or two. But hundreds! That's way too many."

"Hundreds? Looks like a million." Jack stood the farthest away, keeping an eye on the undulating floor. "Did you get stung?" Jack looked him over.

"I'm good." Eagle inspected his legs. "I'm good." He took another deep breath.

"Yeah, you really kept your cool in there," Kay said. She gave him a hug.

Eagle embraced her back.

They all stood at the entrance watching the tarantulas swarm out of the machine and over the floor.

"There's no way I'm going back in there," Jack declared.

"I'm with you. And I was behind that thing." AJ cringed. "Did we get everything out?"

"Yes," Kay said. She looked into the chamber. "But the valve's still open." Hundreds of spiders were swarming over that exact spot.

"Should we leave it on?" Eagle asked.

"What choice do we have?" Jack replied. "The whole chamber's crawling with spiders. Are you seriously going to go back in and shut it?"

Eagle shook his head.

AJ interjected, peering in from around the corner. "I think it's okay. It's just spinning harmlessly. Nothing's happening. Plus, we can't wait here all day for those spiders to clear out. We need to head back home before it gets dark. Let's figure out a plan to get back in there tomorrow and get the machine working."

"You're right, AJ," Eagle said. "It's not doing much, and we'll be back." Eagle paused, then added, "And I'll be wearing my long pants!"

They all laughed.

"Okay, I guess we should head back down." Kay rearranged her pack. "There's not much else we can do." She felt dejected.

They all lowered their heads and started their journey back down the mountain.

⊛ CHAPTER 29 ⊛

The friends headed back down.

"I can't believe we're going to have to make another trip up here," AJ said. "And Eagle, what are we going to do about the spiders?"

"I'm not sure," Eagle replied. "Maybe my grandfather knows a remedy."

They walked solemnly, contemplating what might lie ahead for them and their town. They travelled down and up the hidden stairway and soon arrived back at the river. Kay walked up the ridge and looked into the basin. "Let's take a break over there by the gate. Maybe we can figure out how it goes up. Plus it's shady." She headed down the embankment. Her friends followed.

After arriving at the gate, AJ shed his backpack. "Should we should tell someone about all this?"

Kay spoke. "If we do that, then we're all done here. This

place will be swarming with people trying to figure out what this thing's supposed to do. And the same thing will happen with the machine up at The Spires." Kay walked over to the broken plank on the lower part of the gate. She poked her head in. "Wow! It's actually glowing down there." She pulled her head back. "I'd love to figure this out ourselves."

They all mulled over Kay's words. She was right. Once the town knew of their discovery, their adventure would be over.

"Let's get back up to The Spires tomorrow—see if we can fix the machine," Jack offered. "If we can't, then we should at least tell Talon what's going on. Maybe he could help us figure out what to do. But for now, let's eat here before we head down." He reached into his bag for some food. "I'm hungry—and thirsty."

They talked over their situation while munching on granola bars.

"This whole thing is pretty crazy, right?" Kay reclined against the gate. "An old legend: The Song of the Mountain." She laughed. "Well, at least we're having fun."

"Fun?" Jack shook his head. "We were just chased out of a room crawling with spiders!"

"Yes," Kay replied, "but we did solve a puzzle that unlocked a secret chamber, and we swung across The Spires. No one I know has ever done that."

"That's true," Eagle smiled. "But I was hoping we could save our town."

"It's not over yet," AJ said confidently. "We'll come back tomorrow. Deal with the spiders and figure this thing out."

Suddenly, Kay lifted her head. "Quiet, everyone. Quiet!"

She strained to listen to a faint sound in distance. "Do you hear that?" She stood up and looked toward The Spires.

Eagle tilted his head to listen, too. Deep sounds echoed throughout the valley and bounced off the steep canyon walls. The sounds intensified as the notes repeated in a chord like pattern.

OOOOM-Boom! OO UHM Boom! Boom! Boom! Boom! Da Boom!

OOOOM-Boom! OO UHM Boom! Boom! Boom! Boom! Da Boom!

"I do hear it!" He stood up. The sounds got louder. "It must be coming from The Spires—the pipes. It's—it's playing a song!"

"'The Song of the Mountain'!" Jack cheered.

They looked above the basin. Steam was being ejected from each spire's top. The sounds rocked their bodies.

"Look at that!" Eagle exclaimed.

They all looked at one another and then they all erupted in celebration. Jack high-fived Eagle, making him wince in pain. Kay hugged everyone, and AJ just smiled.

"We got it to work!" AJ declared. "Can you believe it? It works!" The sounds intensified further.

"How's it working?" Jack asked. "Why now?"

"Maybe the spiders' nest was blocking the pipes?" AJ guessed. " Or maybe it just needed some time for the pressure to build up and for the spiders to clear out."

"But what does it do?" Kay shouted over the booming. "And what's with this gate? I'm confused."

The tones increased in intensity. They filled the valley with vibrations. They became so overwhelming that they all covered their ears.

"It's getting way too loud!" Eagle shouted. "Something's happening." He heard cracking noises. Then a feeling of dread washed over him. "Oh no," he gasped.

The whole basin started to shake. Bits of rock broke off the cliffs above the river. Suddenly there was a horrific *crack*. A huge section of the cliff had broken off. Boulders rolled down the steep embankments.

"Avalanche!" Kay yelled.

The friends watched in horror as it all crashed into the river with a thunderous roar.

Water splashed up in a tidal wave and shot out in all directions. Rocks rolled into the basin. AJ, Jack, and Eagle pressed up against the gate to shield themselves.

Kay, at the edge of the gate near the broken plank, reached for her pack to protect herself from the flying rocks. The whole area shook violently—like in an earthquake. She jumped through the broken plank of the gate to take shelter. Still holding her pack, she struggled to maintain her balance. She stumbled and fell. She grabbed the edge of the broken wood, but the shaking made it difficult to hold on.

Eagle bolted over to help. He saw her clinging for dear life just inside the gate. He reached in, but he was too late. He saw Kay tumble backward down the hot shaft. "Kay!" he shouted. Panic gripped him as he watched her slip away.

⊛ CHAPTER 30 ⊛

Kay jammed her palms and soles against the rocky sides of the hot shaft to slow her descent. She desperately tried to find something to grab. The rocks scraped her as she tumbled down, clutching the slightest ledges as they jutted out. She snagged one for a few seconds but then slipped again. As she fell, the air got hotter, the light brighter. She fumbled for her backpack, grasping for something inside.

"Kay!" Eagle screamed through the gap in the gate, but there was no answer. Desperate to save her, he pushed himself through the opening head-first. The area was still shaking. He lost his balance and tumbled into the shaft. His arms were outstretched as he slid down the steep slope, his speed accelerating. There was nothing for him to hold to break his fall. The shaft widened, and he bumped against its rock walls as he fell. The heat intensified, and the glow at the far end became brighter. He couldn't slow himself down. He shrieked as he saw a precipice in front of him, dropping further than he could see. He closed his eyes tight, anticipating a horrible end. Then, suddenly, his shoulder was violently jerked upward. He came to an abrupt halt. Confused, he opened his eyes.

"Kay?" Eagle was disoriented. She was clutching his arm. He breathed heavily.

Kay was clinging to the silver spike with one hand. Her feet were balancing on a narrow ledge.

"Climb up!" she grimaced. "To the spike. Now!" she shouted. "I can't hold you."

Eagle lunged for the silver icicle wedged into a crack right above Kay's head. Shaking off panic, Eagle followed Kay's direction and shimmied up. She let out a deep breath as his weight transferred.

"You okay?" She sized him up. He was a little scraped and bloody from all the tumbling.

Eagle nodded. "Yes," he exhaled deeply. "I thought you were gone"—his voice cracked—"and me, too."

"Yeah, I know what you mean." Kay clung tightly and looked toward the steep drop-off only a few yards away. "I grabbed the spike out of my pack while I fell and dug it in as hard as I could. I couldn't slow down. Then it got caught in this crack. It almost yanked my arm off when it stuck." She laughed slightly. "But I'll take it."

"What now?" Eagle shimmied into a more stable position.

"We'll be okay," she reassured him. "We're not going anywhere. We just need to make contact with Jack." She shared the spike with Eagle and placed her other hand in a crack. Both of their footholds were secure. "Can you reach my phone in my pocket?" She repositioned her body slightly. "I can text him."

Eagle carefully reached around and secured the phone. Kay typed with one hand. *"We r ok...Need rope!"*

"That should do it." She waited for a reply. Moments later her phone buzzed. She looked and then chuckled.

"What's it say?" Eagle asked.

Kay shared the text. *"After I save u I'm gonna kick yur butts!"*

"He's on his way." She grinned.

"Should I be worried?" Eagle asked.

"No. He's just kidding"—she paused—"maybe."

Eagle chuckled. He realized that they'd just dodged a huge bullet. "This is unbelievable." He paused and looked at Kay. "Do you think we're in trouble? Half the mountain just crashed into the river. That can't be good."

"Yeah. But at least we're safe. Right?" She shifted her hands to get a tighter grip.

While they waited for the rope, clinging to the spike, they surveyed their surroundings. "What is this place?" Eagle saw the dim glow radiating from over the steep embankment. The underground crevasse appeared endless. "It must go down for miles."

Kay agreed. "It's hot down there, too." Sweat rolled down both their faces.

"AJ would love to see this," Eagle marveled. "A passageway directly into the Earth."

"You're right. But I'm sure he could do without the falling," Kay said.

"That's for sure." Eagle nodded.

The two braced themselves against the warm rock, waiting to be rescued. Then they heard Jack's voice. "Kay! Eagle!" Their names echoed down the shaft.

Relief washed over Eagle's face.

They both shouted at the top of their lungs. "We're down here, Jack! We're down here!" They clung tight, knowing they were going to be rescued soon.

Eagle caught Kay's eye. "By the way, thanks for saving me. I was really scared."

"Me too, Eagle." She turned away. "Me too."

⊛ CHAPTER 31 ⊛

With AJ securing the rope, Jack rappelled down to find Kay and Eagle. He carefully descended through the shaft. The glow from below illuminated his path. He caught sight of their silhouettes sharing a small ledge. He made his way down and connected them to his rope. Jack instructed Eagle to climb up. Kay followed, ascending the steep shaft until they both poked their heads out through the plank and into the open air. Moments later, Jack crawled out of the opening. He spied Kay on her back, gazing up at the sky.

"Good to see the sun again," she joked as Jack appeared. She looked up at the basin wall. "No more music?"

"That stopped about five minutes ago," AJ said. "It was really loud then tapered off. Are you guys okay?"

Eagle was next to her, getting some water from AJ's canteen. "That wasn't fun." He was exhausted, sweaty, and dirty. "We almost fell to the center of the Earth." He tended to his cuts and bruises.

"Could you see a bottom?" AJ asked.

"I couldn't." Eagle shook his head. "But then again, my eyes were shut." He smiled.

Jack scolded Kay. "You gave me a heart attack! I keep telling you not to take crazy chances."

Kay took a sip of water. "Hey, I was just looking for shelter. And I didn't cause that avalanche."

"That's true." Jack exhaled deeply. "I was really freaked out. We thought you both were gone."

"I know. That was scary. But I also know we all have each other's back." She looked at her friends. "That's what make us a great team."

"So what'd we miss?" Eagle asked. "You said the tones and rumbling stopped a few minutes ago?"

"Yes." AJ looked up the wall of the basin. "But we should go. If the music starts up again, so will the shaking. We've had way too much excitement for one day." AJ grabbed his gear.

"You're right. We need to go," Jack said. "But let's check out the river first—see what happened with the cliff falling into it."

Kay motioned for them to go ahead. "We'll follow in a minute. I'm gonna help Eagle bandage his arm." She reached into her pack for her first-aid kit and passed it over. She then repacked the silver spike into one of the front pockets of her pack.

Jack and AJ climbed up the steep embankment to the crest overlooking the river. From there they saw the damage from the rockslide. Boulders, smaller rocks, and mud littered the channel. White-capped waves flowed swiftly over the larger stones. AJ looked to the chokepoint—the spot where the cliff walls abutting the river narrowed. It was completely blocked! Water was backing up behind the blockage as if it were a dam. He realized that soon the river would overflow the low ridge, sending water cascading over the banks and down into the basin below.

AJ looked back toward his friends still at the bottom of the basin. "Get out!" He shouted. "Now!" The river was rising at an alarming rate.

"What now?" Eagle groaned. He and Kay grabbed their packs and raced up the ridge. Eagle hustled to keep up with Kay.

"Run faster!" AJ yelled. Eagle could hear panic in his voice.

Kay and Eagle bolted up the embankment. Just as they were halfway up, they heard the rush of water above them. Seconds later, droplets sprayed over the crest, soaking them.

"What's going on up there?" Kay called.

"The water is backing up at the chokepoint," Jack shouted. "It's gonna overflow. You need to move it!" He watched in horror as the water breached the ridge and rushed downward toward Kay and Eagle.

The flood hit Kay first and then Eagle, knocking them off balance. They tumbled back down into the basin. The water was now up to their knees. They sloshed through the current, trying to fight their way out. Then Kay looked up to the ridge and saw a wall of water crashing toward them.

"Run!" she yelled to Eagle. But they couldn't. The force of the current was too strong. They labored through the water, struggling to escape. Eagle looked back at the wall of water surging over the ridge and braced for its impact. It swept him up and carried him as it flowed in a giant whirlpool around the basin.

AJ and Jack stood helpless on the ridge as they watched Kay and Eagle struggle in the whirlpool below. Jack reached into his pack and pulled out his rope. He tied a quick knot, like a lasso. He prepared to throw it down into the rising water. Kay and Eagle were bobbing up as they circled the basin at different points in the rising flood.

The water rose quickly. Kay's pack weighed her down, but she could not remove it: The current was too strong. Kay caught site of Jack with his rope at the top of the cliff. She saw him fling it. She lunged for it but missed. The current dragged her away.

Eagle too was swept along by the whirlpool. He spied the rope and flailed to grab it as he came around. He too missed.

"Darn it!" Jack pulled in the rope, preparing for another attempt.

The water level was now halfway up the gate. The current was spinning them as if they were in a washing machine.

Jack coiled the rope. Trying to time his throw, he hurled the rope directly in Kay's path, right as she was coming around. She struggled for it but missed again. She hoped Eagle would have better luck.

"Just stay on top," AJ called. He studied the advancing water in the basin. The water level had risen almost fifty feet. It was now only a few yards below the river. As it reached the river's level, the current slowed dramatically. Kay and Eagle were still spinning around, but the full basin was now more like a lake.

Feeling the drop-off in the current, Kay and Eagle swam toward each other.

"I think we're okay now," Eagle exhaled as they met up. "We just rose fifty feet." He looked across the water. They were only a few yards below the level of Jack and AJ standing on the ridge. Eagle looked in the opposite direction. The huge gate was now completely submerged. Even the side columns that rose a few feet above the top of the gate were underwater.

Relief washed over Jack and AJ.

"I guess that worked out," AJ said. "Throw them the rope and help them out of there."

Jack reset the rope and tossed it into the calmer water. It splashed a few yards from their position.

Kay reached for the rope. "Got it," she exulted.

Eagle clung to her as Jack reeled them both in.

"That was scary," Eagle admitted. They splashed through the water with Jack's assistance toward the bank. "I'm glad that's over."

"Yeah," Kay breathed heavily. "I guess that's what the Tectonic legend meant by reshaping the land." She swam on her side, struggling with the weight of her pack. "Let's get out of here. What crazy thing can happen next?"

Just as she uttered those words, a rumble and creak sounded from the cliff just above the submerged gate.

Eagle caught Kay's eye. "What's happening?" His heart pounded.

The rumble intensified. Rocks broke loose and splashed into the water from above the gate. Then the gate popped up from under the water like a float. They watched in astonishment as it rose up on its tracks.

⊛ CHAPTER 32 ⊛

A giant vortex swirled in the middle of the water-filled basin. The spinning water rushed down the funnel and through the passageway that had opened behind the gate.

Eagle and Kay were still clinging to the rope. It pulled tight toward the vortex as the current grabbed them. The sudden jolt tore the rope through Jack's hands. He screamed as the rope burn stung him.

"Pull the rope, Jack," AJ yelled. "You've got to get them out of there!" He lunged for the rope to help.

"I'm doing it!" Jack's voice cracked. He winced in pain as he fought the current. Needing to get better leverage, he crouched down, wedging his feet behind a rock. He dug in for a long battle.

"How did the gate rise up?" Jack grimaced.

AJ helped Jack with the rope. He looked over to the gate. The tops of each of its side columns were now just above the water line. The gate was floating! "The air. It's trapped in the columns. Those must be buoys! That's what keeping it up." AJ had an idea. He left Jack and bolted toward the gate.

"Where are you going?" Jack screamed at him. "I need your help!"

"I have to close the gate!" AJ shouted back. He darted along the top of the basin to the opposite side. As he ran, he watched Kay and Eagle fight the current—clutching the rope—hoping that they and Jack could hold on. Within moments he had arrived at a point above the gate. He scrambled down the rocks, trying to get to one of the side buoys.

Struggling to keep afloat, Kay and Eagle spied AJ as he scrambled down to one of the side columns. They saw him jump onto one.

"What is he doing?" Kay shouted. "Why isn't he helping Jack?" She turned to Eagle. "Don't let go." She yelled over the rushing water. "Just hold on. Jack's got us."

"But it's sucking us in!" Eagle gasped for air. He put his head down on Kay's pack and held on for dear life.

Kay looked over to Jack. "Pull!" she screamed.

Jack hunkered down behind one of the rocks along the cliff wall. He gritted his teeth. His biceps bulged as he struggled to fight the swift current and hold Kay and Eagle's weight. The rope was stretched tight, as he was unable to take in any slack. He wasn't sure how long he could hold on.

The gate was up, suspended on its tracks along the side cliff like a garage door. He now understood why the two side columns rose a few feet above the top of the gate. They trapped in more air to offset its enormous mass so it could float in the water.

Thousands of gallons of water gushed into the passageway beneath, left open by the floating gate. AJ jumped into the water and with one arm held tight to one of the side columns. With the other arm he tried to pry off the round wooden top. He realized that if he could pop the top off like a cork, the hollow column would fill with water and lose its buoyancy. AJ found the seam. He wedged in his fingers, frantically scraping and scratching to pop it loose. Panic gripped him as he failed to get any leverage.

Over the rushing water, Eagle watched AJ and figured out what he was trying to do. With all his energy, he screamed to him over the loud rush of the water. "What's wrong?"

Hearing Eagle's cry, AJ yelled back. "It's stuck!" He scraped at the seam again.

"What's he trying to do?" Kay gasped. Her body was stretched between the rope she was holding and the vortex sucking her down.

"He's trying to shut the gate by filling the hollow sides with water." Eagle fought the current, still clutching onto Kay's pack. "The lid's stuck."

"Stuck?" Kay's eyes lit up. She had an idea. "Eagle, get the spike from my pack. It's in the front pocket. Throw it over to him."

Eagle understood. "That's perfect!" The silver spike would act like a crowbar, enabling AJ to pry up the lid. Fumbling under the water, Eagle unzipped the pocket and grabbed the spike. Mustering all the energy he could, he prepared to throw it over to AJ. He was at least thirty feet away.

"You can do it," Kay encouraged. "This is the ultimate

carnival game." Kay craned her head around to see Eagle make the throw. "But do it quick. And don't miss. I don't know how long Jack can hold us."

"AJ!" Eagle called. "Heads up!" He heaved his arm back and grunted as he thrust his body forward. Propelled through the air, the silver spike tumbled, end over end, toward the gate. AJ, seeing the sharp object heading straight for him, ducked out of its way. It landed like a dart in the column's cap.

AJ jumped on top of the column and wiggled the spike free. He held it like a knife and wedged the point into the seam. He jiggled it back and forth, so it stuck. He stood upon the column and knocked the spike in further with his shoe. Once the spike was secure, he jumped back into the water and clung to the column's side. He pulled down on the spike, using it like a crow bar to push the lid up. A small gap opened. He slid the spike around the seam, opening the gap wider. When the spike had gone about halfway around, he was able to squeeze his whole hand in. He took a deep breath and pushed up. The lid popped off.

Holding on to the column, AJ frantically splashed water inside. As it filled up, the gate lurched downwards creaking and rumbling. Within seconds, the hollow tube had filled.

"Yes!" AJ exulted. "It's working!" The gate was sliding back down.

The weight of the water sent the one side crashing down on its track. The gate listed to one side. Now it was stuck—half open.

"Do the other one!" Eagle shouted. The spinning vortex was still sucking down thousands of gallons of water into the passageway beyond the gate, but Kay and Eagle could feel that the force of the current had been reduced.

With the spike in his hand, AJ climbed out of the water and leaped to the other column. He repeated the process, wedging in the spike all around the edge of lid until he was able to pop it off. As he splashed water in, the column got heavier and started to sink. When its top became level with the water line, the hollow structure completely filled up, forcing the gate down. It closed with a loud thud.

⊛ CHAPTER 33 ⊛

The gate was now shut. The spinning vortex was gone, so Jack was able to pull Kay and Eagle to shore. However, water still flowed from the river into the basin.

Kay and Eagle now lay on the dry land, exhausted. Jack's hands were bleeding. AJ made his way over and joined them.

"This has become way too dangerous," Kay admitted. She gulped down deep breaths. "Thanks for saving us, guys. That was quick thinking with the gate, AJ. And Jack...."

"I know." Jack cut her off. "Don't worry about it."

'Yeah, big guy." Eagle rolled on to his back. The sun was drying his clothes. "Thanks for holding on to us. We would have been sucked down to the center of the Earth."

Jack smiled. "Believe me. I know. That's the second time I've saved your butts in the last hour." He chuckled. Jack grabbed some gauze from one of the packs. He rolled it around his sore hands. Red blood soaked through. "All kidding aside,

Kay's right: this has become way too dangerous."

"We should get out of here," AJ said. "Who knows what will happen next? We clearly started some kind of chain reaction."

"Do you think we're going to get in trouble?" Eagle got to his feet. "That river supplies all the water for the town. It's completely cut off. And look at this"—he pointed to the water-filled basin—"What about all that water that went through the gate? What's going to happen with that?"

"We should tell Talon," Kay said. "He'll understand. Right, Eagle?"

Eagle pondered Kay's suggestion. He was concerned about getting into trouble, but he knew she was right. "I think so," Eagle agreed.

"Okay, let's go." AJ said. He walked over to Kay. "And here"—he handed her the silver spike—"I'm glad you brought this." He smiled.

"Me too," she laughed. "And good throwing, Eagle. You're definitely ready for the carnival."

The friends were anxious to leave. Just as they took one step, the ground beneath them shook.

"Oh no. What now?" AJ scanned the valley.

"Take cover!" Jack shouted. They all ducked down, seeking shelter behind anything they could find.

The shaking turned to a rumble and then suddenly a thunderous clap: *Ka-boom!* Peering over the ridgeline, they all witnessed the north slope of Mount Fuego erupt. The whole side blew off. Red-hot lava spewed from newly formed cracks. The thunderous roar echoed through the valley.

After a few seconds the shaking stopped. They got to

their feet and saw the thick, glowing of lava flowing harmlessly into the northern valley. The river of red covered the black rock, following the same path as it had hundreds of years earlier. They looked at one another in awe.

"Is this good?" Jack hoped. "The whole mountain just exploded."

"I think it is!" AJ exulted. "It's just like those fracking stories in the news. The injected water causes the bedrock to shift." He gazed at the glowing lava field. "It must have pressurized somehow and that blew off the side of the mountain."

"That sure explains why people are concerned about fracking," Kay said. "It really did reshape the landscape."

"It looks exactly like the pictures on the walls of the spire cavern." Eagle paused, looking at his friends. "I think we just saved our town! Just like the Tectonic did hundreds of years ago."

There was a moment of silence, and then they all broke into shouts of joy.

"We saved our town, and we had no clue as to what we were doing!" Eagle joked. They all laughed uncontrollably.

"Sure, we almost got swept to the center of the Earth, twice, but we made it out, right?" Kay high-fived everyone.

For some time, from their position overlooking the basin and river, they watched the glowing lava flow through the valley.

"Do you really think this will reduce the pressure that was causing the earthquakes?" Kay asked.

"It's got to," AJ replied. "Like you said a long time ago: just like removing the cap off a shaken soda bottle."

"What about the river water that the town needs?" Jack worried. "That's still a big problem. It's all backed up."

AJ looked down into the basin. It was still filling up with water, but the gate was not going to open this time. The water-filled columns would keep it down. "Hold on, guys." He got everyone's attention. "Check out the water." From his vantage point, he could see clearly how the next few minutes would play out. "This is gonna be unbelievable." He urged them to move up onto the highest ledge between the basin and river.

With the gate shut, the water continued to rise. It overflowed the basin and spilled back over the ridge and into the river. The water level and pressure rose behind the blockage that the avalanche had created. Rocks, boulders, and mud crunched together as the pressure built. Suddenly water forced its way through tiny gaps in the dam. A few small rocks were propelled outwards. *Pop, pop, pop!* Then a trickle of water, followed by a stream, and finally a torrent crashed through the barrier. The flow of water resumed down the main river canyon, making its way toward their town.

⊛ CHAPTER 34 ⊛

"**I**'ll take the funnel cake." AJ handed the money to the vendor. He shared his treat with Kay. It was a few days later, and they were back at the amusement park. They had just gotten off The Flush ride.

"So which is scarier?" AJ ripped a piece of dough and put it in his mouth. "That ride or being sucked down into the center of the Earth?" he joked.

"I think you know the answer to that," Kay replied. She snagged a piece of cake. She enjoyed feeling the sugar dissolve on her tongue.

"They keep playing the news clip about the lava flow," AJ said. "No one knows what we did—except Talon. But they say everything is good. We don't have to leave."

"Isn't the whole thing incredible?" Kay smiled. "Like Eagle said, we didn't even know what we were doing." She laughed.

"We'd get into so much trouble if our parents knew what we did," AJ said. "My mother wouldn't let me out of the house for years."

"I know what you mean." She nodded. "But it all worked out." She looked into the crowd. "Hey, let's go find Jack and Eagle. They're probably at the games."

As they walked, Kay spotted two large stuffed animals bobbing through the crowd: a giant tarantula and a rattlesnake. They were heading straight for them. Then she spotted Eagle holding them. He was grinning as he made his way over.

"They cut me off." He held both prizes high in the air. "They told me I couldn't play any more. Two's the limit."

"He's really good." Jack was proud. "I taught him everything he knows." He put his arm around him.

They both chuckled.

"Where's yours, Jack?" Kay tilted her head. "There was no way you didn't win one."

"I gave mine to that girl over there." Jack waved.

"Naturally," Kay smirked.

"And this one, Kay." Eagle held out the tarantula. "This one's for you."

Smiling wide, she gladly accepted it. "I'll hang it up with my silver spike!"

Jack reached for some of the funnel cake left in AJ's hand. AJ smiled and shook his head.

"Hey, now that everything's back to normal, do we need to go back to The Spire cave?" Jack chewed his treat. "You know, deal with the spiders and turn the machine off?"

Eagle stepped forward. He repositioned his prize so he

could see Jack. "No need. Kay and I went back a couple of days ago."

"What?" Jack said. "Where was I?"

"You were working," Kay reminded him. "Remember all those people in town to study the lava flow? Dad's restaurants are booming."

"Oh yeah." Jack nodded. "They tip well."

"We knew we needed to go back and turn it off—just to be safe," Eagle said. "The spiders were all gone, so it was pretty easy."

"How about the key to the secret chamber at the mesa?" AJ asked.

"We gave it to Talon," Kay said.

"Yeah, that's right." Eagle confirmed. "He's going to check it out with his friends. He said they'll pass down the stories of our adventure for generations." Eagle huddled everyone together. "He was so proud of all of us." He scanned their faces. "So proud. He knew we would save the town."

"Well, I guess everything is back to normal," Jack said. "Are you guys all ready for Devil's Drop? AJ, you in this time?"

"After what we've been through?" AJ looked slightly annoyed at even being asked. "You bet!"

"Great!" Jack put his big arm around AJ. "But I stand corrected. Things are not normal if you're up for this." Jack laughed. "All right, guys. Let's do it. Devil's Drop." Jack led the way.

The friends reread the warning sign at the base and laughed:

Do not go on this ride if you have a fear of heights, a heart condition, a back condition, or any other ailment that might cause you to freak out while being hurled a hundred feet down toward the ground! Good luck and have fun!

"I do have a fear of heights, but I'm not going to freak out." AJ sounded confident. "I've been on worse."

"We all have," Eagle affirmed.

Kay and Eagle handed their prizes to the ticket-taker for safekeeping. Then the four friends bounded up the staircase, quickly covering the one hundred feet to the platform. When they arrived, the attendant gave them their harnesses. "Do you guys know how these work?"

They laughed. "Yes, we do," Kay answered for them all.

"Check it out." Kay pointed toward town. "There's the wind sculpture. The tiles are so glittery—even from up here." She looked over to Eagle. "Remember, you still need to make something for Ms. Lody." She chuckled.

"Yeah, I know." Eagle shook his head. He tapped AJ on the shoulder. "You're going to help me, right?"

"What was that?" AJ smiled.

Eagle groaned.

They all laughed.

The attendant connected the rope swing to their harnesses using carabiners. "You guys are all set. Get ready to jump off on the count of three."

The friends moved into position at the edge of the platform.

"*One.*"

"Everybody ready?" Kay called.

They all nodded.

Eagle looked out to The Spires in the distance. "Just like before, AJ. Enjoy the ride."

"*Two.*"

The friends all bent their knees.

AJ's heart pounded. He smiled at his friends and they all smiled back.

"Let's do it." Jack squeezed everyone tight.

"*Three.*"

They leaped off the platform into the open air.

They soared.

The End.

ACKNOWLEDGMENTS

Writing is a collaborative process. I'd like to thank all the people who have helped me craft this story and enabled me in countless ways.

To Kayla and Jackson for inspiring me to write this book by providing countless suggestions and motivating me to continue.

To my editor, Judith, who challenged me to make the story better at every juncture.

To my friends Dee Dee, John L, John S, Randy, Chris M, Nichole, Bridget, Scott I, Felicia and Augie who encouraged me, checked in on my progress, and helped me work out important details while I was formulating and writing the story.

To Steve L and my friends from college, Dave H, Chris, John, Veronica, Dave Y, Kate, Karen, Stephanie, Linda, and Mike for sharing many of the New Mexican settings with me.

To my proofreaders' David R, Josie, Betsy L, Lisa P, and Marge who helped sharpen the story line and provided invaluable suggestions.

To Dionne B who coordinated the book cover contest and assisted in finalizing the look and feel of the book.

To the teachers, staff and friends at the Winchester Thurston School, Ashley, Gary, David P, Joan, Callie D, Karen G who provided inspiration, guidance and support from the beginning of the project through to its conclusion.

To the artists from the Winchester Thurston School, Lily, Coco, Sophia, Crystal, Lorin, Patrick, and Katharine who are all so talented and helped bring to life the settings and cover art.

To the parents, friends, families, and coaches of my children's soccer and hockey teams for showing genuine interest in my endeavor and who put up with me talking about this book for a year!

And to my wife, Amy, who believed in me and supported this effort from the beginning. This book would not have been written without you.

Thank you all!

Alan Zemek wrote his second book, *The Magma Prophecy*, by drawing on his life experiences. He met his wife while rock climbing and is the father of two adventurous kids. The family travels together all over the world and explores sites in depth by going on scavenger hunts. They enjoy outdoor activities, including kayaking, climbing, biking, and hiking.